By the end of the week, he felt as wound up as a coiled spring.

There were several women he could call—casual mistresses who would be happy to join him for dinner at an exclusive restaurant followed by a night together, with no strings attached. So why wasn't he tempted to pick up the phone?

The answer could be found in a pair of grey eyes that regarded him coolly across the dinner table every evening. Sometimes the expression in those eyes was not as dismissive as he suspected their owner wished. Emma was fighting the chemistry between them. But it was there, simmering beneath the surface of their polite conversation, and blazing in the stolen glances they shared. He heard her swiftly indrawn breath when he leaned close to refill her wineglass, and he knew they both felt a tingle of electricity when their hands accidentally brushed.

Their attraction to one another was undeniable, but for the first time in his life Rocco could not simply take what he wanted.

CHANTELLE SHAW lives on the Kent coast, five minutes from the sea, and does much of her thinking about the characters in her books while walking on the beach. An avid reader from an early age, she found that school friends used to hide their books when she visited, but Chantelle would retreat into her own world, and she still writes stories in her head all the time.

Chantelle has been blissfully married to her own tall, dark and very patient hero for over twenty years and has six children. She began to read Harlequin® romance novels as a teenager, and throughout the years of being a stay-at-home mum to her brood, she found romance fiction helped her to stay sane! Her aim is to write books that provide an element of escapism, fun and of course romance for the countless women who juggle work and a home life and who need their precious moments of "me" time. She enjoys reading and writing about strong-willed, feisty women and even stronger-willed sexy heroes. Chantelle is at her happiest when writing. She is particularly inspired while cooking dinner, which unfortunately results in a lot of culinary disasters! She also loves gardening, taking her very badly behaved terrier for walks and eating chocolate (followed by more walking—at least the dog is slim!).

Other titles by Chantelle Shaw available in ebook:

Harlequin Presents

Harlequin Presents Extra

A DANGEROUS INFATUATION

CHANTELLE SHAW

~ Irresistible Italians ~

TORONTO NEW YORK LONDON
AMSTERDAM PARIS SYDNEY HAMBURG
STOCKHOLM ATHENS TOKYO MILAN MADRID
PRAGUE WARSAW BUDAPEST AUCKLAND

Recycling programs
for this product may
not exist in your area.

ISBN-13: 978-0-373-52850-9

A DANGEROUS INFATUATION

First North American Publication 2012

Copyright © 2011 Chantelle Shaw

www.Harlequin.com

Printed in U.S.A.

A DANGEROUS INFATUATION

CHAPTER ONE

SNOW had been falling across Northumbria all day, burying the moors beneath a thick white blanket and icing the peaks of the Cheviot Hills. Picturesque it might be, but it was no fun driving on slippery roads, Emma thought grimly as she slowed the car to a crawl to negotiate a sharp bend. With the onset of dusk the temperature had plummeted to well below freezing, and most of the minor country lanes had not been gritted, making journeys treacherous.

The north-east of England often saw snow in the winter, but it was unusual to last this late into March. Thankfully, her battered old four-by-four, which had once seen service on her parents' Scottish hill-farm, coped well with the conditions. It might not be the most stylish vehicle, but it was practical and robust—rather like her, Emma acknowledged, with a rueful glance down at the padded ski jacket she was wearing over her nurse's uniform. The jacket made her resemble a beach ball, but at least it kept her warm, and her thick-soled boots were sturdy and sensible.

The narrow road wound uphill, bordered on either side by the walls of snow that had been piled up when a farmer had cleared the route with a tractor earlier in the day. Nunstead Hall was still three miles ahead, and Emma was growing concerned that even if she made it to the isolated house she was in danger of being stranded there. For a moment she contemplated turning back, but she hadn't visited Cordelia for two days, and she was anxious about the elderly lady who lived alone.

A frown furrowed her brow as she thought of her patient. Although Cordelia Symmonds was in her eighties she was fiercely independent. But six months ago she had fallen and broken her hip, and then recently she had had an accident in the kitchen and badly burned her hand. Cordelia was becoming increasingly frail, and it was no longer safe for her to live alone at Nunstead, but she had refused to consider moving to a smaller house closer to the village.

It was a pity Cordelia's grandson did not do more to help his grandmother, Emma thought darkly. But he lived abroad, and always seemed too busy with his high-powered career to have time to visit Northumberland. She had heard the pride and affection in Cordelia's voice on the many occasions when she had spoken of her grandson, but sadly the old lady seemed to have been abandoned by her only living relative.

It wasn't right, Emma thought fiercely. The subject of care for the elderly was close to her heart—particularly after the terrible event at the beginning of the year when she had visited a ninety-year-old man and discovered he had passed away in his armchair in a freezing cold house. His family had gone away for Christmas and had not arranged for anyone to check on him. The thought of the poor man dying alone still haunted her.

Remembering Mr Jeffries, Emma knew she could not allow the situation with Cordelia to continue. Perhaps she could somehow contact Cordelia's grandson and persuade him that he needed to take some responsibility for his grandmother? she brooded.

The car slid on the icy road, and she concentrated on driving through the increasingly heavy snowfall. It had been a long and difficult day, due mainly to the weather. Just this last visit, she thought wearily, and then she could collect Holly from the childminder, go home to the cottage and light a fire before she started cooking dinner.

She chewed on her lip as she recalled how her daughter had been coughing again when she had dropped her at nursery that morning. Her flu virus had been particularly severe, and the long winter wasn't helping the little girl to pick up. Spring couldn't come soon enough. Warm sunshine and the chance to play outside in the garden would do Holly the world of good, and hopefully put some colour back on her pale cheeks.

Rounding the next bend, Emma gave a startled cry when she was faced with car headlights blazing in front of her. Instantly she braked, and let out a shaky breath when she realised that the other car was not moving. A quick inspection of the scene told her that the car must have skidded on ice, spun around and then hit the bank of snow at the side of the road. The back end had actually crashed through the snow wall, and was partly submerged in the ditch.

There only seemed to be one occupant—a man—who flung open the driver's door and climbed out, apparently unhurt.

Halting her car beside him, Emma leaned over and wound down the window.

'Are you all right?'

'*I* am, but that's more than can be said for my car,' he replied tersely, his eyes on the sleek silver sports car half buried beneath a mountain of snow.

His voice was deep-timbred, with a faint accent that Emma could not immediately place but sent a tiny frisson down her spine. It was a very sexy voice—as rich and sensuous as molten chocolate. She frowned at the unexpected turn of her thoughts. A practical and down-to-earth person, she was not prone to wild flights of fancy.

The man was standing to one side of his car, out of the glare of the headlights, so she could not make out his features. But she noted his exceptional height. He was easily several inches over six feet tall. His superbly tailored sheepskin coat emphasised the width of his broad shoulders. Although she could not see him clearly, she sensed his air of wealth and sophistication, and she wondered what on earth he was doing in this remote area. The nearest village was miles back down the road, whilst ahead stretched the vast Northumberland moors. She glanced down at his leather shoes, which were covered in snow, and immediately dismissed the idea that he might be a hiker. His feet must be freezing.

Even as the thought came into her head he stamped his feet, as if to get the blood circulating, and pulled a mobile phone from his pocket.

'No signal,' he muttered disgustedly. 'Why anyone would choose to live in this godforsaken place is beyond me.'

'Northumbria is renowned for its unspoilt beauty,' Emma felt compelled to point out, feeling a tiny spurt of irritation at his scathing tone.

In her opinion, anyone who chose to drive across the moors in a snowstorm should have the sense to pack a spade and other emergency supplies. Personally, she loved Northumberland's dramatic landscapes. When she had been married to Jack they had rented a flat in Newcastle, but she hadn't enjoyed living in a busy city and had missed the wildness of the moors.

'There are some wonderful walks through the National Park—although it is rather bleak in the winter,' she conceded. Sensing the man's impatience, she continued, 'I'm afraid my phone doesn't work out here either—few of the phone networks do. You'll have to get to a village before you can call a garage, but I doubt anyone will send a truck to tow your car out until tomorrow.' She hesitated, instinctively wary of offering a complete stranger a lift, but her conscience nagged that she could not leave him stranded. 'I've got one more visit to make and then I'll be going back to Little Copton, if you want to come with me?'

He had no choice but to accept the woman's offer, Rocco realised as he walked around his car and saw that the back wheels were submerged in three feet of water. Even if he could clear the mound of snow that had collapsed on top of the roof, it would be impossible to drive up the side of the ditch; the wheels would simply spin on the ice. There was nothing for it but to find a hotel for the night and arrange for his car to be rescued in the morning, he concluded, reaching over to the back seat to retrieve his overnight bag.

He glanced at the bulky figure of the woman in the four-by-four and guessed that she was from one of the farms. Maybe she had been out to check on livestock: he couldn't imagine why else she would be driving across the moors in the snow.

She was certainly well built, he thought, as he climbed up into the car and squashed himself into the small space on the seat beside her. But her woollen hat was pulled low over her brow, and a thick scarf covered most of the lower half of her face, so it was impossible for him to guess her age.

'Thank you,' he murmured, closing the door and feeling a welcome blast of warm air from the car's heater. It was only now sinking in that he was lucky not to have been injured in the crash, and that he could have faced a long, cold walk to find civilisation. 'I was fortunate you were driving this way.'

Emma released the handbrake and carefully pulled away, her hands tightening on the steering wheel when she felt the car slide. She rammed the stiff gear lever into second gear, and tensed when her hand brushed against the man's thigh. In the confines of the vehicle she was even more aware of his size. His head almost brushed the roof, she noted, darting him a lightning glance. The collar of his coat was pulled up around his face, hiding his features, so that all she could really see of him was the dark hair which fell across his brow.

In the warm car the spicy scent of his cologne teased her senses. It was an evocatively masculine smell and stirred an unbidden memory of Jack. Her mouth tightened as the image of her husband's handsome face, his shock of blond hair and his lazy grin, flooded her mind. Jack had been a natural-born charmer who had loved the finer things in life, she remembered bleakly. She had bought him his favourite, ruinously expensive aftershave the last Christmas they had spent together, naively unaware that he probably wore it when he slept with other women.

She slammed a brake on her thoughts and became aware that the stranger was staring at her.

'What did you mean when you said you have to make one last visit? It's not a good night to be out socialising,' he said, glancing through the windscreen at the snowy lane illuminated by the car's headlights.

The area was familiar to Rocco. He knew there was only one more house ahead before the road dwindled to a track that wound across the moors. It was a stroke of good luck that his rescuer was heading in the direction of his destination, but he was puzzled as to where she was going.

Once again Emma felt a little quiver run down her spine

at the man's husky, innately sexy accent. Definitely not French, she decided, but possibly he was Spanish or Italian. She was curious to know why he had been driving along a remote Northumbrian country lane in a snowstorm. Where had he come from and where was he heading? But politeness and her natural diffidence prevented her from asking him.

'I'm a district nurse,' she explained. 'One of my patients lives out here on the moor.'

Beside her, she felt the stranger stiffen. He snapped his head towards her and seemed about to say something, but at that moment a stone gateway loomed out of the darkness.

'Here's Nunstead Hall,' Emma said, relieved to have arrived in one piece. 'Enormous, isn't it? The grounds are beautiful, and there's even a private lake.'

She turned onto the driveway and stared up at the imposing old house that was in darkness apart from one window, where a light was shining, and then glanced at the forbidding stranger, wondering why he made her feel uneasy. His brows were drawn into a deep frown, and she was puzzled by his tangible tension.

'Does your patient live here?' he demanded tersely.

It was too dark to see the expression in his eyes, but something about his hard stare unnerved her.

'Yes. You can probably phone the garage from the house,' she told him, assuming that he was frowning because he was anxious about his car. 'I have a door key so that I can let myself in. I think it would be better if you stay here while I ask Mrs Symmonds if you can use the phone.'

She reached over to the back seat for her medical bag and seconds later felt a blast of cold air rush into the car. 'Hey!' Irritation swept through her when she saw that the stranger had ignored her instructions and climbed out of the four-by-four. He was already striding up to the front door of the Hall, and she hastily jumped out and ran after him, stumbling in the thick snow that covered the ground. 'Didn't you hear what I said? I asked you to stay in the car. My patient is elderly and might be frightened at the sight of a stranger on the doorstep.'

'Hopefully I'm not that terrifying a sight,' he drawled, sounding arrogantly amused. He brushed off the snow-flakes that were settling thick and fast on his coat. 'Although if you don't hurry up and open the door I'm going to look like the Yeti that's reputed to stalk the Himalayas.'

'It's not funny,' Emma snapped. She did not care for the hard glitter in his eyes, and wished that instead of rescuing him from the roadside she had phoned Jim at Yaxley Farm, which was the closest neighbour to Nunstead Hall, and asked him to bring a tractor to tow the stranger's car out of the ditch. She gave a startled gasp when the man took the key from her fingers and slotted it into the lock. Her anger turned to unease. For all she knew he could be a criminal on the run, or a lunatic! 'I must *insist* that you return to the car,' she said firmly. 'You can't just stroll in as if you own the place.'

'But I do own it,' he informed her coolly as he pushed open the door.

For a few seconds Emma gaped at him, stunned, but when he stepped across the threshold into the house she regained the use of her tongue. 'What do you mean? Who *are* you?'

She broke off when a door leading off the hallway opened and tiny, silver-haired Cordelia Symmonds appeared. Desperately concerned that the old lady would be scared to find a stranger in her home, Emma spoke quickly.

'Cordelia, I'm so sorry—this gentleman was stranded in the snow and...'

But Cordelia did not appear to be listening. Her eyes were focused on the stranger and a beaming smile spread across her lined face.

'Rocco, my darling. Why didn't you tell me you were coming?'

'I wanted to surprise you.' The man's accented voice was suddenly as soft as crushed velvet. 'Unfortunately my car skidded on ice, but luckily the nurse here—' he flicked a sardonic glance at Emma '—offered me a lift.'

Cordelia did not seem to notice Emma's confusion. 'Emma, dear—what a wonderful girl you are for rescuing my grandson.'

Grandson! Emma's eyes flew to the stranger. In the brightly lit hall she could see his face clearly, and she recognised him now. Pictures of him frequently appeared in celebrity gossip magazines, alongside frenzied discussion about his tangled love life. Rocco D'Angelo was the CEO of a famous Italian sports car company—Eleganza— and a multi-millionaire playboy who was reputed to be one of Europe's most eligible bachelors. And Cordelia's grandson.

Why hadn't it clicked? Emma asked herself impatiently. The clues had been there—the flash car, his foreign accent and his indefinable air of *savoir-faire* that only the very rich possessed. She hadn't been expecting to meet him, of course. But why hadn't he explained who he was? she thought irritably.

'Come along in, both of you,' Cordelia invited, turning back to the sitting room.

Emma went to follow, but found her way barred as the stranger—she was still struggling with the shock news that he was Cordelia's grandson—stepped in front of her.

'Just a moment—I'd like a word with you. Why exactly are you here?' Rocco asked in an undertone, pulling the sitting room door half closed so that his grandmother could not hear their conversation. 'Cordelia looks perfectly well. Why does she need a nurse to visit her?'

It was there again—that faintly haughty tone in his voice that made Emma's hackles rise. Images flashed in her head of poor Mr Jeffries, who had died alone, and Cordelia's joyous smile at her grandson's unexpected visit. The elderly lady clearly thought her grandson was Mr Wonderful, and from his arrogant air Rocco D'Angelo seemed to share that opinion.

'If you took *any* interest in your grandmother you would know why I am here,' she said sharply, feeling a small spurt of satisfaction when his eyes narrowed. 'I don't know if you're aware that Cordelia fell and broke her hip a few months ago. She's still recuperating from hip replacement surgery.'

'Of course I know about that.' Rocco disliked the nurse's belligerent attitude, and the implicit criticism of him that was apparent in her tone. His voice iced over. 'But I understood that she was recovering well.'

'She's over eighty, and she should not be living here in this remote house all alone. Her recent accident when she burned her hand is proof of that. It's a great pity that you are too busy with your own life to pay Cordelia any attention.' Emma gave him a scathing look. 'From what I understand, you are her only living relative. You should be doing more to help your grandmother.' She pushed past him. 'Now, please excuse me. I need to see my patient.'

The sitting room was like an oven. At least Cordelia did not stint on heating the house, Emma thought, watching Rocco—who had followed her into the room—immediately shrug off his coat. Her eyes seemed to have a magnetic attraction to him, and she felt a peculiar sensation in the pit of her stomach as her brain registered that he was utterly gorgeous. His black jeans and matching fine wool sweater moulded his lean, hard body. Raven-dark hair was swept back from his brow, emphasising the perfect symmetry of his chiselled features, his sharp cheekbones and square chin giving him a harsh, autocratic beauty that took her breath away.

With his incredible looks he could be a film star, or a male model from one of those glossy magazines that were occasionally donated to the surgery's waiting room and featured articles about the rich and famous aboard their yachts in Monaco, she brooded.

He looked over at her, and she felt embarrassed that he had caught her staring at him. Her face grew hotter when he trailed his unusual amber-coloured eyes over her in brief assessment, before dismissing her with a sweep of his thick black lashes. Clearly he did not consider her worthy of a second glance. But why would he? she asked herself irritably. She was not a skinny, glamorous clothes horse like the stunning French model Juliette Pascal, who was reputed to be his current mistress. Emma had long ago accepted that even if she dieted permanently she would never be a fashionable and totally unachievable size zero, and she was painfully conscious that in her padded jacket she looked like a sumo wrestler.

Rocco was seething. The gratitude he had felt towards the nurse for rescuing him from the roadside had rapidly disappeared when she had voiced her opinion that he did not care properly for his grandmother. She knew nothing about his relationship with Cordelia and had no right to pass judgement on him, he thought furiously.

He adored his *nonna*, and the nurse's assertion that he was too wrapped up in his own life to pay her any attention was ridiculous. However busy he was, he always phoned her once a week. It was true he hadn't managed to come to England for quite a while—not since his brief visit at Christmas. He felt a pang of guilt when he realised that it was nearly three months since he had last been at Nunstead.

But Cordelia did not live alone. The nurse—Emma, he recalled his grandmother had called her—was wrong about that. Before he had returned to Italy he had employed a housekeeper to take care of the house *and* Cordelia.

Thoroughly riled, he glared at Emma, whose face was still half hidden beneath her scarf. Never in his life had he seen a woman wear such an unflattering hat, he mused, his eyes drawn with horrible fascination to the red woollen monstrosity on her head, which had slipped so low that it now covered her eyebrows. But she was no longer looking at him, and was staring down at Cordelia's feet.

'Cordelia, why is there snow on your slippers?' Emma frowned when she saw the elderly lady shiver. 'Don't tell me you've been outside in the garden? It's freezing, and you could have slipped on the ice.'

'Oh, I only went a little way down the path.' A worried look crossed Cordelia's face. 'Thomas has disappeared. I can't find him anywhere.'

'I'll look for him, and then I'll make some tea. You sit by the fire and warm up,' Emma instructed firmly, concern for her patient providing a welcome distraction from Cordelia's disturbingly handsome grandson.

In the kitchen she filled the kettle and then opened the back door. The garden was a white wilderness illuminated by the moonlight. She compressed her lips at the sight of footsteps across the snow-covered lawn. Thank heavens Cordelia hadn't fallen; hypothermia would have set in very quickly in the sub-zero temperature.

Gleaming green eyes caught her attention. 'Thomas, come here you little pest.' A ball of ginger fur shot past, but she managed to catch it, wishing she was still wearing her gloves when the cat dug his needle-sharp claws into her hand. 'It would have been your fault if Cordelia had slipped over,' she told the animal with mock sternness.

Her expression became serious. This situation could not be allowed to continue. For her own safety Cordelia would have to be persuaded to move closer to the village—or her arrogant grandson who had turned up out of the blue would have to be persuaded to take responsibility for his frail grandmother, and at the very least arrange for full-time staff to care for her at Nunstead Hall.

Rocco D'Angelo was in the kitchen when she went back inside. Although the room was a fair size it suddenly seemed claustrophobically small as he prowled around like a sleek, dark panther. Even his name was sexy, Emma thought ruefully, irritated with herself for the way her heart-rate quickened when he strode around the table and halted in front of her, his glittering golden eyes trapping her gaze.

'Who is Thomas?' he demanded curtly. 'And why are *you* making tea? Surely the housekeeper should do that?'

'This is Thomas.' Emma set the cat on the floor. 'He turned up on the doorstep a couple of weeks ago and Cordelia adopted him. We think he'd been abandoned and had been living wild, but sought shelter when the weather became colder. He's half feral and usually only goes to your grandmother,' she added, glancing at the scratch on the back of her hand and feeling a flare of annoyance when Thomas rubbed his head against Rocco's leg and purred. 'And there isn't a housekeeper, as I'm sure you know,' she continued sharply. 'To be honest, I don't know how you can have allowed Cordelia to remain here when there's no one to help with shopping and cooking, and generally keeping an eye on her. I'm sure you lead a very busy life, Mr D'—'

'I hired a housekeeper called Morag Stewart to look after the house *and* my grandmother the last time I was here at Nunstead.' Rocco interrupted the nurse mid-flow. It was obvious she had been itching to give him a lecture on his inadequacies, but he was in no mood to listen.

He was well aware of his failings, he thought grimly. As always, coming back to Nunstead Hall evoked memories of Giovanni. It was twenty years since his younger brother had drowned in the lake on the grounds of the house, but time had not erased the memory of his mother's hysterical screams, nor her accusation that it was *his* fault Gio was dead.

'I told you to look after him. You're as irresponsible as your goddamned father.'

The image of his brother's limp, lifeless body still haunted him. Gio had only been seven years old, while Rocco had been fifteen—old enough to be left in charge of his brother for a few hours, his mother had sobbed. He should have taken better care of Gio. He should have saved him. But he had failed.

Rocco's jaw tightened. The guilt he felt about Gio was now mixed with a new guilt that once again his actions had resulted in terrible consequences—although mercifully not in another death. But it had been a close call, he acknowledged grimly. A year ago a young actress, Rosalinda Barinelli, had swallowed an overdose of sleeping pills after he had ended their affair. It had only been by lucky chance that a friend had found her and called an ambulance. Rosalinda had survived, but had admitted that she had tried to take her life because she could not bear to live without *him*.

'I always wanted more than an affair, Rocco,' she had told him when he had visited her in hospital. *'I pretended to be happy as your mistress, but I always hoped you would fall in love with me.'*

To his surprise, Rosalinda's parents had been sympathetic when he'd explained that he had been unaware of their daughter's feelings, and that he had never made promises of marriage or commitment to her. They had revealed that Rosalinda had formed a similar strong attachment to a previous boyfriend. She had always been emotionally fragile, and they had not blamed Rocco for her suicide attempt. But, despite the Barinellis' reassurance, he still blamed himself.

Now, as he stared at Emma, his conscience pricked. Maybe she was right to be concerned about his grandmother. He could not understand why Cordelia was living alone at Nunstead Hall, but he was determined to find out what was going on.

CHAPTER TWO

EMMA switched the kettle onto boil and began to unravel her scarf. Glancing down, she saw that she had walked snow into the kitchen from the garden, and tugged off her boots before unzipping her jacket. Her mind dwelled on Rocco D'Angelo's assertion that he had arranged for a housekeeper to work at Nunstead.

'There's never been a housekeeper here since I've known Cordelia. I've never met this Morag Stewart, and your grandmother has never mentioned her. When did you say you hired her?'

'Just before Christmas.' Rocco's jaw hardened at the scepticism in Emma's voice. He was infuriated that she clearly did not believe him. He was not used to having his actions questioned—especially by a woman. In Rocco's experience women agreed with everything he said.

'Nonna was still frail after her hip replacement. I wanted to take her to my home in Italy, but she refused to leave Nunstead. You might be aware that I am the chief executive of the sports car company Eleganza?' he continued coldly. 'It is a demanding job and I have little spare time.'

The past four months had been manic. The death of his father after a short illness had been a shock, and his workload had been immense as he had continued to run

Eleganza at the same time as trying to sort out Enrico's affairs. What a tangled web his father had left behind, Rocco thought grimly.

He stared at the nurse through the cloud of steam that enveloped her as she poured water from the kettle into a teapot. 'I knew I would not have time to visit England regularly, so I contacted a staff agency and subsequently appointed Morag Stewart as housekeeper and companion to Cordelia.'

'Your grandmother didn't become my patient until the end of January,' Emma said slowly. The realisation was sinking in that she might have misjudged Cordelia's grandson. 'I took over caring for her from one of my colleagues after our rounds were reorganized, and I was immediately concerned that she lived on her own such a long way from the village. At first I only saw her once a week, to check her blood pressure, but since she burned her hand I've visited every couple of days.' She stared at Rocco, accepting that it was unlikely he had made up the story about hiring a housekeeper. 'Morag Stewart must have left Nunstead for some reason,' she ventured.

'I intend to find out *why* from Cordelia.'

But his intention to quiz his grandmother about her unsatisfactory living arrangements was not as imperative as it had been a few moments ago, Rocco discovered. Ever since he had watched Emma pull off her boots, to reveal a pair of surprisingly shapely legs sheathed in black hose, he had been intrigued to see the rest of the woman who had so far been hidden by outerwear that would not have looked out of place in the Arctic. The removal of her scarf had exposed a face far younger than he had expected, with creamy skin and a lush, full-lipped mouth that drew his gaze.

Now she pulled off her hat and shook her head, so that

her hair settled around her face in a chin-length strawberry blonde bob that shone like raw silk beneath the bright kitchen light. Her features were attractive rather than pretty, Rocco mused. There was strength in the firmness of her jaw, and her grey eyes, the colour of rain-clouds, were intelligent and coolly assessing. Finally she shrugged off her padded jacket. Her body was an even more pleasant surprise, he noted, skimming his eyes over her blue nurse's uniform and focusing on her slim waist, the gentle flare of her hips and the rounded fullness of her breasts.

The thought came into his head that this was how a woman *should* look. He was jaded by a diet of whippet-thin, glamorous models. Emma's curvaceous figure was a delightful contrast to his numerous high-maintenance mistresses. As he stared at her he was reminded of a Renaissance painting of Adam and Eve in the Garden of Eden. Like Eve, Emma's soft curves were sensual and tempting. He wondered what she looked like naked, imagined her breasts filling his hands like plump peaches…

The sharp stab of desire in his groin was unexpected and disconcerting. She wasn't his type, he reminded himself. To his surprise he found her physically attractive, but her brisk, no-nonsense personality reminded him of the strict headmistress of the English prep school he'd been sent to at the age of six, and her readiness to jump to conclusions without checking facts irritated the hell out of him.

Which brought him back to his grandmother and the case of the missing housekeeper, he brooded.

'I still think you should have found the time to visit between Christmas and now.'

The nurse's disapproving voice interrupted Rocco's thoughts.

'If you had, you would have known the housekeeper

wasn't here and that Cordelia was struggling to cope on her own. I appreciate that you lead a busy life, Mr D'Angelo, but I know for a fact that you aren't always working. Cordelia saves every newspaper clipping about you, and only last week she showed me a photo of you on the ski slopes at Val d'Isère.'

Emma opened a cupboard and took down three of the bone china cups and saucers that she knew Cordelia preferred to mugs before turning to face Rocco.

'In my opinion…'

'I'm not interested in your opinion,' he stated. 'Particularly in relation to my private life.' Rocco's mouth thinned as he struggled to control his anger. What would the sanctimonious, busybody nurse say, he brooded, if he revealed that the reason for the skiing trip had been an attempt to build a relationship with his father's illegitimate young son, Marco—a half-brother whose existence he had been unaware of until shortly before Enrico's death? 'My personal life is no concern of yours.'

'True,' Emma agreed tightly. 'But your grandmother's welfare *is* my concern. I'm worried about her safety, living on her own, and I'm sure she's not eating properly. I would be failing in my duty if I did not report my concerns to Social Services.'

She could tell from the dangerous gleam in Rocco's tiger-like golden eyes that she had angered him with her bluntness. In her job she had found that people often became defensive when reminded of their responsibilities towards a vulnerable relative. But it was too bad, she thought, lifting her chin to meet his intimidating glare. She had grown very fond of Cordelia, and dreaded the thought of her falling and lying unaided, because there was no one around to come to her rescue—just as no one had come to the aid of poor Mr Jeffries.

'Your grandmother needs help,' she told Rocco fiercely. 'It is unacceptable for you to abandon her while you gallivant around the world—whether for business or pleasure,' she added, thinking of the attractive blonde in the photo, who had no doubt been Rocco's companion both on and off the ski slopes.

Rocco muttered a curse under his breath, his patience finally snapping. 'I head a billion-dollar global company. I do not *gallivant* anywhere. And I have certainly not abandoned Cordelia.' He took a deep breath and sought to control his temper. Emma was a nurse, he reminded himself, and it was her job to ensure that her patient was safe and well cared for. 'I appreciate your concern, but it is unnecessary. I am perfectly capable of looking after my grandmother.'

'Really?' Emma's brows arched disbelievingly. 'I've seen little evidence of that. Cordelia has been struggling for weeks—the accident when she burned her hand was very serious. Your turning up out of the blue occasionally is simply not good enough. What she needs is for you to live here at Nunstead with her.'

'Unfortunately that is impossible. Eleganza is based in Italy and I need to live there.' Even more so now that he had Marco to consider, Rocco thought heavily. But he was damned if he would explain himself to Miss High-and-Mighty. All Emma needed to understand was that he intended to fulfil his responsibility towards his grandmother and take care of her—although quite how he was going to do that when Cordelia had always insisted that she would never leave Nunstead Hall was something he had not yet figured out.

It was not surprising that Rocco preferred to live at his luxurious villa in Portofino rather than on the wind-swept Northumberland moors, Emma thought, recalling the photos of his house in the Italian province of Genoa that Cordelia had once shown her. There had been other photographs of Rocco aboard his yacht, with the sea sparkling in the background and a gorgeous brunette in a minuscule bikini pressing her body seductively up against him.

'My grandson is a handsome playboy, just like his father,' Cordelia had said, her obvious fondness for Rocco mixed with a faint air of resignation at his pleasure-seeking lifestyle. 'But he says he has learned from his father's mistakes and has no intention of marrying and having children.'

Emma dragged her thoughts back to the present. 'Well, something has got to be done,' she said crisply, trying to dismiss the memory of the photo and Rocco's muscular, tanned torso from her mind.

She had finished making the tea and went to pick up the tray at the same time as he stretched his hands towards it. Heat shot up her arm at the brush of his warm skin against hers. Startled by the unexpected contact, and her reaction to it, she jerked her hand away as if she had been burned.

The kitchen door swung open and Cordelia walked in, seeming not to notice Emma's pink cheeks or the way she quickly stepped away from Rocco.

'I was wondering what had happened to the tea,' the elderly lady said cheerfully.

'I was just about to bring it in.' Nothing in Rocco's voice revealed that he was fighting a strong urge to run his fingers through the shiny bell of red-gold hair that framed Emma's face. He could not identify her perfume, but he liked the delicate lemony fragrance, which was so subtle compared to the cloying designer scents most women he knew chose to drown themselves in.

With an effort he dragged his mind from the sexual allure of his grandmother's nurse and fixed Cordelia with a stern glance. 'Nonna, where is the housekeeper I arranged to live at Nunstead with you?'

'Oh, I sacked Morag ages ago—after I discovered her stealing money from my purse,' Cordelia told him brightly. 'Dreadful woman—I'm certain she had been pilfering from almost the minute she arrived. I've realised since she left that several pieces of silverware have disappeared.'

Rocco exhaled heavily. 'Why didn't you tell me? You knew I did not want you to live alone after your fall last year.' His exasperation with his grandmother was mingled with a flare of satisfaction when he noted the guilty expression on Emma's face. She knew now that he had not abandoned Cordelia. Perhaps that would teach her to be a little less judgemental in future, he thought self-righteously. On the other hand, his conscience pointed out, Emma *had* been right when she had said that he should have found the time to visit Cordelia during the past three months.

'I didn't want to worry you,' his grandmother explained. 'You had enough to deal with, running Eleganza. And of course losing your father must have been such a shock.' She sighed. 'It's hard to believe that my one-time son-in-law is dead. Enrico can only have been in his early sixties, and he was still so handsome. He had just finished making another film when his cancer was diagnosed, hadn't he?'

Rocco nodded. 'At least he was not ill for very long. He would have hated that.' His father had not been an easy patient, he remembered heavily. Enrico D'Angelo had been one of Italy's most famous film stars. Fêted and adored all his adult life, he had expected his son, for whom he'd had little time during Rocco's childhood, to be at his bedside twenty-four hours a day. But there had been little that Enrico's doctors could do apart from keeping the dying man comfortable, and Rocco had felt a sense of helplessness that he could not save his father—just as he had not saved his brother, nor prevented his mother's fatal accident years before.

Dragging his mind from the past, Rocco recognised his grandmother's attempt to steer the conversation away from herself. 'But, Nonna, I wish you had told me about the housekeeper. I believed these past few months that you were being looked after.'

'I don't *need* looking after,' Cordelia argued hotly. 'You should know by now that I'm a tough old stick. And before you start—' she fixed her grandson with a sharp stare '—I will not move from Nunstead. I was born here, and I intend to die here.'

Emma glanced at Rocco and felt a reluctant tug of sympathy for him. His grandmother was barely five feet tall, and looked as though she weighed little more than a sparrow, but she was as strong-willed as an ox. Rocco would have a battle on his hands if he attempted to persuade Cordelia to move house, she thought ruefully.

He turned his head and their eyes met in a moment of mutual understanding. She knew she owed him an apology. It sounded as though he had done his best to arrange a live-in companion for Cordelia, and far from being too busy to come to England he had remained in Italy to be with his terminally ill father.

'Why don't we go back into the sitting room?' she murmured, addressing Cordelia because she felt embarrassed about how unfairly she had accused Rocco. 'I want to take a look at your hand.'

It was a relief to move away from the gorgeous Italian. She was shaken by her strong awareness of him. He made her feel flustered and on edge, and caused her heart to thud unevenly. But *why* did he have such an effect on her? she asked herself impatiently as she followed him along the hall, trying not to allow her eyes to focus on his muscular thighs and the taut buttocks outlined beneath his close-fitting black denim jeans. He was stunningly good-looking, but she knew of his reputation as an inveterate charmer, and she had sworn after Jack that never again would she be seduced by a handsome face and a ton of charisma.

As they neared the door to the sitting room she glanced at the portrait of Cordelia's daughter hanging in the hallway. Flora Symmonds had been exquisitely beautiful, she mused as she studied the painting of the world-famous actress who had died unfairly young and at the height of her career.

'She was stunning, wasn't she?' Rocco halted next to her and followed her gaze. 'My dear *mamma*—beautiful, talented, but unfortunately a lousy mother,' he said harshly.

Emma gave him a shocked look. 'You don't mean that.' She was glad Cordelia had walked ahead of them into the sitting room and could not hear her grandson.

'It's the truth.' Rocco's jaw hardened as stared at the portrait of his mother. 'Both my parents were selfish and self-obsessed. They should never have had children, and they quickly realised that fact and sent us away to school as early as possible.'

'Us?' Emma was puzzled. Cordelia had only ever spoken of Rocco, as if he was her only grandchild.

He was silent for so long that she thought he was not going to answer her, but then he said quietly, 'My younger brother and I attended boarding school in England. Cordelia was more of a parent to me than either my mother or father. I spent many school holidays here at Nunstead when my parents were both away making films.' He turned his head from his mother's picture and gave Emma an amused smile. 'I agree that the Northumberland National

Park has some great walks. I spent a lot of time exploring the moors when I was a boy.'

Emma felt her face redden at his reference to their conversation in the car, when she had been unaware of his identity. 'I didn't realise you were familiar with the area,' she muttered, adding a touch defensively, 'It's a pity you didn't explain who you were.'

He shrugged. 'I did not know you were on your way to visit my grandmother and saw no reason to introduce myself. I see now that your concern for Cordelia was justified,' he added honestly. 'If I had known she was living alone I would have immediately come to England and made other arrangements regarding her care.'

She believed him. The affection Rocco felt for his grandmother was evident in his voice, and Emma felt ashamed of the way she had been so quick to judge him. 'I'm sorry about your recent bereavement,' she mumbled. 'I hadn't made the connection, until Cordelia spoke of him, that Enrico D'Angelo was your father. He was a brilliant actor. I was shocked when I read about his death in the newspapers a few months ago.'

Although Rocco did not appear to have been close to his parents, it must be hard to have lost both of them, she thought. She guessed he was in his mid-thirties, which meant he would have only been a young man when his mother had driven her car along a clifftop road on the French Riviera and taken a hairpin bend too fast.

The accident had made headlines around the globe. Flora Symmonds and Enrico D'Angelo had been world-famous film stars whose tempestuous marriage, numerous affairs and bitter divorce had been played out in the media spotlight. It was little wonder that Rocco had preferred to spend his school holidays with his grandmother, in the peaceful surroundings of Nunstead Hall.

Her eyes strayed against her will to his sculpted face. He met her gaze, his golden eyes gleaming, and her heart gave a little flip when his mouth curved. She might have known that his smile would be devastatingly sensual. He was the archetypal alpha-male—good-looking, confident and oozing sex appeal. Just like Jack, and exactly the type of man she had vowed to avoid like the plague.

The timely reminder of her husband served as a cold shower, dousing her awareness of Rocco. He was a charmer, but she was determined not to be charmed, and her smile was distinctly cool as she murmured, 'I think you had better carry the tea in before it stews.'

Five minutes later Rocco grimaced as he watched Emma remove the dressing on Cordelia's hand to reveal a large patch of raw scarlet skin. 'That looks painful,' he said grimly. 'How did you burn yourself, Nonna?'

'Oh, the silliest thing.' Cordelia shook her head impatiently. 'I had heated up some soup for my lunch and somehow managed to spill it onto my hand while I was pouring it into a bowl. Those copper-based saucepans are terribly heavy. I shall buy some different ones the next time I go to Morpeth.'

'How have you been getting to the town, or even Little Copton, since Morag left?' Rocco frowned as he thought of how isolated his grandmother was here at Nunstead Hall. One of the reasons he had appointed Morag Stewart had been because she had assured him she would be happy to drive Cordelia around the local area.

'I haven't been able to go anywhere since Dr Hanley said that my eyesight is too poor for me to be able to drive. I'm sure he's wrong,' Cordelia said indignantly. 'I was perfectly safe. I used to drive ambulances in London during the Blitz, you know.'

'I know you did, Nonna. You were—and are—amazing,' Rocco said softly.

Cordelia's spirit was as indomitable as ever, but her reference to the part she had played in the Second World War was a reminder of her advancing years, he thought heavily. Once again he felt guilty that he had not checked to see that all was well at Nunstead Hall, but he had been so focused on his father in the weeks before he died, and also on searching for Enrico's mistress, who was the mother of his young son.

'I'm very lucky to have such a wonderful nurse,' his grandmother continued. 'Emma has been bringing me my shopping. I don't need much—just milk and bread mainly—but I must have cat food for Thomas. He does like his three meals a day.'

'He's the best fed cat in the whole of Northumberland,' Emma said dryly. 'I only wish *you* would eat three meals a day, Cordelia.'

There was genuine affection in her voice, and the smile she gave his grandmother was notably warmer than the frosty glances she occasionally directed his way, Rocco noted. Although he hated to admit it, his curiosity was piqued by Emma's coolness. It was fair to say that it was not the sort of response he usually received from women, he thought self-derisively.

He acknowledged his luck in having been blessed with an athletic build and facial features that had drawn attention from the opposite sex since he was a youth. A degree of cynicism, developed over the years, warned him that his status as heir to his grandfather's billion-pound company added greatly to his appeal. Mistresses came in and out of his life with mundane regularity, and it was rare for any woman to hold his interest for more than a few months.

It was always too easy, he reflected. He had never met a woman yet who had presented a challenge.

His eyes were drawn again to Emma's neat red-gold bob that curved around her face. There was nothing frivolous about her appearance. Her practical hairstyle was the ideal choice for a busy professional, yet there was something very sexy about her sleek, shiny hair that made him want to run his fingers through it.

Eliciting a smile from her could be an interesting challenge, he mused. His gaze lingered on her mouth, and the unbidden image came into his head of tasting her, of slanting his lips over hers and exploring their moist softness. She was sitting on the sofa, attending to Cordelia's hand, but she looked up at that moment and Rocco was startled to feel heat surge into his face.

Dio, the last time he'd felt embarrassed was when he had been fourteen and the housemaster at his boarding school had caught him looking at pictures of half-naked women in a magazine. Muttering an oath beneath his breath, he strode over to the window to close the curtains, grateful for the excuse to turn his back on his grandmother's nurse while he fought to bring his libido under control.

Emma finished re-bandaging Cordelia's hand. 'The burn is healing slowly, but there's still a risk of infection so you need to keep it covered for another few days. I'll visit again on Monday to change the dressing,' she said as she stood up.

Her body tensed involuntarily when Rocco strolled across the room and halted beside her. Although she carefully did not look at him, she was supremely conscious of him towering over her, and to her disgust her hand shook slightly as she closed the zip of her medical bag.

'It's started snowing again,' he announced. 'The roads were treacherous on the way here, and they can only be worse now. I think it would be a good idea for you to spend the night here, Emma.'

His sexy accent lingered on each syllable of her name and sent a little quiver of reaction down Emma's spine. For heaven's sake! How could she be seduced by his *voice*? ~~she berated herself silently.~~

Taking a deep breath, she flashed him a polite half smile. 'Thanks for the offer, but I must get back.'

Rocco frowned. In his mind he had pictured sitting by the fire with Emma after his grandmother had retired to bed, enjoying the particularly fine malt whisky Cordelia always kept for him and exerting his acknowledged easy charm to break through her barriers. Her crisp refusal shattered the cosy picture and aroused his curiosity.

'Is someone expecting you?' This blunt question was just about the most unsubtle way of discovering if she had a partner, he acknowledged sardonically.

'My three-year-old daughter.' Cool grey eyes briefly met his gaze before flicking to the clock on the mantelpiece. 'I was due to collect Holly half an hour ago. Fortunately her childminder was fine about it when I phoned to explain that I would be late. But now I really must go.'

'Can't your daughter's father collect her?'

Rocco did not know who was more surprised by his unguarded query—him or Emma. He couldn't understand what had got into him—or why, when he glanced at her left hand, the sight of the gold wedding band on her finger intensified his feeling of irritation.

'No.' Emma did not offer any further explanation. The mention of Holly had made her impatient to get home. She was aware of Rocco's frown, but she had no intention of appeasing his idle curiosity by discussing Holly's father. 'I'll just go and get my boots and jacket, and then I'll be off. Stay in the warm, Cordelia,' she added, when the elderly lady began to get to her feet. 'I'll see you after the weekend.'

'Don't forget your hat,' Cordelia called after her. 'It's lucky I knitted it for you. You need it in this weather.'

Emma stifled a sigh at the mention of the dreaded woollen hat that so resembled a tea cosy. But Cordelia had been so proud when she had presented it to her a few weeks ago that she'd felt she must wear it. As she passed Rocco she caught the glimmer of amusement in his eyes and flushed.

He was waiting by the front door when she walked back down the hall from the kitchen a few minutes later. She was desperately conscious of his appraisal and, although she knew she was being ridiculous, she wished she was wearing her elegant grey wool coat rather than the unflattering ski jacket.

'I'll see you out,' he said, opening the door so that a gust of icy air rushed into the hall. The snow falling from the inky black sky was light, but steady, and not for the first time that winter Emma was grateful to her father for giving her the four-by-four.

'There's no need for you to come out,' she told Rocco when he followed her down the front steps.

He ignored her and walked with her to where she was parked. 'I haven't thanked you for coming to my rescue.' His face was shadowed in the darkness, but his eyes glowed amber, reminding her once again of tiger's eyes.

'You're welcome.' Emma hesitated. 'To be honest, I'm relieved you're here. I worry about Cordelia living alone in such a remote place. How long do you plan to stay?'

'I'm not sure yet.' His original intention to visit his grandmother for a few days was no longer viable, Rocco acknowledged. But he could not remain in England indefinitely when he had a business empire in Italy to run.

Perhaps Emma recognised his quandary, because after

she had climbed into the four-by-four she gave him a sharp look. 'While you're here I'll need to arrange a meeting with Social Services so that we can decide on the best way to care for Cordelia.'

Her schoolmistress tone annoyed Rocco. Did she think he would simply disappear and abandon his grandmother? He was about to tell her that he did not need interference from her or anyone else, but then remembered that without Emma's help over the past weeks Cordelia might have come to serious harm.

He gave a brief nod. 'You had better get going before the snow gets worse. Will you phone to say you have arrived home safely, to put my grandmother's mind at rest?'

The journey back to Little Copton on the hazardous roads demanded Emma's full attention, and she pushed all thoughts of Rocco D'Angelo to the back of her mind.

'I'm sorry I'm so late,' she apologised to Holly's child-minder when Karen opened the door of her bungalow and ushered her inside. 'The roads are like a skating rink.'

'Don't worry about it. Holly has been fine playing with the twins,' Karen reassured her. 'I gave her dinner with Lily and Sara, but she didn't eat much, and she looks tired now. That flu virus really knocked her out, didn't it? What the two of you need is a nice, relaxing holiday— somewhere abroad, where it's warm and sunny.'

'Some hope,' Emma said with a sigh. 'My finances simply won't stretch to a foreign holiday, and I can't plan anything while the owner of Primrose Cottage is considering putting it up for sale. I might have to start looking for somewhere else to live.' Her heart sank as the worry that had gnawed away at her for the past few weeks filled her mind, but her smile was determinedly bright when she walked into Karen's sitting room and Holly hurtled into her arms.

'Mummy, I missed you.'

'I missed you too, munchkin.' More than words could convey, Emma thought silently as she lifted her daughter into her arms and hugged her tight.

Leaving Holly every day was a wrench she had never grown used to, but she had no choice. She enjoyed her job as a nurse, but when she had fallen pregnant she had planned to take a career break for a few years to be a full-time mother. Fate had intervened, and the necessity to pay rent and bills meant that she had returned to work when Holly had been six months old. It also meant that the time she spent with her daughter was doubly precious, and her heart ached with love when Holly pressed a kiss to her cheek.

'Let's go home,' she said softly, trying not to think about the possibility that Primrose Cottage might not be their home for much longer.

Holly was half-asleep by the time Emma had driven through the village and parked outside the cottage. Deciding to forgo giving the little girl a bath, she quickly carried out the routine of pyjamas, teeth cleaning and bed-time story, and then tiptoed from Holly's bedroom. An omelette was not a substantial meal after a long day at work, but it was all she could be bothered to cook for her dinner. But first she needed to phone Nunstead Hall to let Cordelia know she was home.

It was ridiculous for her pulse-rate to quicken as she made the call, but to her annoyance she could not control it—nor prevent the lurch of her heart when a gravelly, ac-cented voice greeted her.

'Emma—I assume you have arrived home safely?'

'Yes, thank you.' Was that breathy, girly voice really

hers? And why did the sexy way that Rocco drawled her name make her feel hot and flustered? A glance in the hall mirror revealed that her cheeks were pink, she noted disgustedly. Having successfully put him out of her head for the past hour, she was dismayed when the image of his arrogantly handsome face filled her mind.

Sexual awareness had taken her by surprise from the moment she had followed him into Nunstead Hall and seen him properly for the first time, she acknowledged ruefully. He had dismissed her at first, after a cursory glance. But later, when she had taken off her coat in the kitchen, he had trailed his mesmeric amber eyes over her in a lingering appraisal, the memory of which sent a quiver down her spine.

Oh, hell. She gripped the phone tighter and fought to control her rising panic. She had never expected to be physically attracted to any man ever again. It was just chemistry, she assured herself. A mysterious sexual alchemy that defied logical explanation. It was inconvenient and annoying, but she was a mature woman of twenty-eight, not a hormonal adolescent, and she refused to allow her equilibrium to be disturbed by a notorious playboy.

'I hope your daughter was not upset that you were late to collect her?'

Once again Rocco's deep voice made her think of rich, sensuous molten chocolate. She drew a ragged breath and by a miracle managed to sound briskly cheerful. 'No, Holly was fine. She's in bed now, and I'm just about to cook my dinner, so I'll say goodnight, Mr D'Angelo.'

'Rocco,' he insisted softly. 'My grandmother has been talking about you all evening. She is clearly very fond of you, and now that I feel I know everything about you it seems too formal to address you as Mrs Marchant.'

'Right…' The word emerged as a strangled croak.

What on earth had Cordelia said about her? Emma wondered, feeling highly uncomfortable with the idea that Rocco knew 'everything' about her. Her flush deepened, and she had a strange feeling that he sensed her discomposure and was amused. She pictured his mouth curving into a slow, sexy smile, and was shocked to feel her nipples harden.

It was suddenly imperative that she end the call. 'Well, goodnight…Rocco.'

'*Buonanotte*, Emma. And thank you again for your help tonight.'

Rocco's expression was thoughtful as he replaced the receiver and strolled back into the sitting room at Nunstead Hall. He could not deny that he was more intrigued by Emma Marchant now he had learned that she was a widow. According to Cordelia, Emma's husband had been dead for three years—yet she still wore a wedding ring. Three years was a long time to grieve, he mused.

His jaw tightened. Why was he thinking about her? Heaven knew he had enough to deal with—including the problem of how he could take care of his grandmother. He did not have the time or the inclination to pursue an inconvenient attraction to a woman who came with baggage that included a young child.

CHAPTER THREE

USUALLY Emma loved Saturday mornings, with their promise of two whole days that she could spend exclusively with her daughter. But the weekend started badly when she picked up the post from the doormat and opened a letter from her landlord, informing her that he had decided to put Primrose Cottage on the market. The two months' notice she had been given to move out was more than Mr Clarke was legally bound to offer, and she appreciated his consideration, but she felt sick at the prospect of uprooting Holly from her home and trying to find somewhere else to live.

'You promised we could make cakes, Mummy,' Holly reminded her over breakfast.

'So I did.' Her appetite non-existent, Emma crumbled her uneaten piece of toast onto her plate, ready to feed the birds, and smiled at Holly's eager face. There was no point in fretting and spoiling the weekend, she told herself.

But the arrival of the estate agent later in the morning to take measurements and photographs of the cottage emphasised the stark reality of the situation.

'There are no other properties to rent in Little Copton, but I have a couple of houses on my books that are up for sale,' the agent told her. 'They're both bigger than this place, though,' he added. 'Four bedrooms, couple of bathrooms and big gardens—they might be out of your price range.'

'I don't have a price range,' Emma said dismally. 'I can't afford the deposit necessary to secure a mortgage. If I could, I'd snap up Primrose Cottage.'

She sighed. Holly was so settled in the village; she attended the local nursery and her name was down for the primary school where all her little friends would go. But now it looked as if they would have to leave Little Copton and move to a town where there were more properties available to rent.

The peal of the doorbell drew a frown. She wasn't expecting any visitors, and her heart sank at the thought that it might be another estate agent come to take details of the cottage.

'You look as though you're having a bad morning.'

Yes, and it had just got a whole lot worse, Emma thought silently, feeling her heart jerk painfully beneath her ribs when she pulled open the door and stared at Rocco D'Angelo's stunningly handsome face. It should be illegal for a man to smile the way he was smiling, with a lazy, sexy charm and a bold gleam in his golden eyes as he subjected her to a leisurely appraisal. His gaze lingered rather longer than was appropriate on her breasts. Perversely, she wished she was wearing something more flattering than a long-sleeved grey jersey top that had shrunk in the wash.

'You seem to have something on your shirt.'

Following Rocco's gaze, Emma glanced down and discovered that her chest was spattered with fine white powder. 'It's flour,' she muttered, blushing as she attempted to brush the flour from her breasts. 'We're baking cakes, and Holly whisked the ingredients a little too enthusiastically.' To her horror she realised that her nipples were jutting provocatively beneath her clingy top. A glance at Rocco's face told her he had noticed, and she quickly crossed her arms in front of her, feeling thoroughly flustered. 'Are you here for a reason, Mr D'Angelo? Because I'm rather busy.'

Dark eyebrows winged upwards at her sharp tone. 'I thought last night that we had agreed on Rocco?' he drawled. 'And, yes, there *is* a reason for my visit. Perhaps you could invite me in so that we can discuss it?'

Rocco glanced over Emma's shoulder into the narrow hallway of the cottage and tensed when a man emerged from a room at the back of the house. Was she busy entertaining a boyfriend at ten o'clock in the morning—or had the guy spent the night with her? For some reason the idea darkened his mood, and that in itself was irritating. He had convinced himself last night that he wasn't interested in his grandmother's nurse. But he had changed his mind when Emma had opened the door, looking delectably gorgeous with her red-gold hair framing her pretty face. Her fitted jeans skimmed the soft curves of her hips, and her too-tight top moulded her full breasts, evoking a hot throb of lust in his groin as he imagined pushing the stretch material aside and cradling the bounteous mounds of flesh beneath.

The last thing Emma wanted to do was invite Rocco into her home, but good manners prevented her from saying so and she reluctantly moved to one side, so that he could step into the hall. He immediately dominated the small space, the top of his head brushing against the wooden ceiling beams that were a feature of the old cottage. He was too big, too dominant and way too overwhelming, she thought, hiding her irritation as the estate agent walked towards them, making the hallway feel even more cramped.

'I've taken all the photos I need.' The agent cast a curious look towards Rocco before focusing his attention on

Emma. 'I like the way you've done the place up. It's fresh and bright and I believe it will sell pretty quickly.'

'I'm in no rush for it to be sold,' Emma said heavily, 'but I expect the landlord will be pleased.' She opened the front door again, to allow the agent to leave, and then turned to face Rocco. He was intruding on her precious time with Holly and she was impatient for him to go. 'What was it you wanted to discuss?'

'Where are you moving to?' Rocco parried her question with one of his own.

She shrugged. 'I don't know. I only heard this morning that the owner has decided to sell Primrose Cottage. I'd like to stay in the local area, but if I can't find somewhere affordable to rent I may have to consider moving closer to Newcastle.'

'Cordelia would miss you if you moved away.'

'I'd miss her, too.' Emma bit her lip at the prospect of having to leave the village she loved and the many friends she had made in the past three years, since she had moved into Primrose Cottage with her month-old daughter. She had built a life for herself and Holly here, away from all the painful memories of Jack.

'Why don't you buy the cottage yourself?' Rocco's voice interrupted her thoughts.

'I'd love to, but it's impossible. I'm a single mother, and my nurse's salary simply won't stretch to buying a house.'

The scent of Rocco's cologne teased her senses, and in the small hall she had nowhere to look but at his broad-shouldered figure. He was dressed in pale jeans and a thick oatmeal-coloured sweater, topped by a black leather jacket; the look was casual yet sophisticated—and heart-stoppingly sexy. Emma resented her fierce awareness of him. She wished he would explain the reason for his unexpected visit, but he seemed in no hurry to leave.

'Cordelia told me your husband died. Did he not leave some sort of provision for you and your daughter such as a life insurance policy?'

Emma almost laughed at the suggestion that Jack might have behaved with any degree of responsibility. In fact she had been awarded compensation from the fire service after his death, but the money had all gone on settling his huge credit card debts that she had been unaware of until she had sorted through his paperwork.

'Unfortunately not,' she said crisply, her tone warning Rocco that it was none of his business. She faced him square on, preventing him from walking down the hall. 'Look, I don't mean to be rude, but I have a lot to do this morning…'

'Mummy, I iced the cakes…'

Emma turned her head and stifled a groan when Holly trotted out of the kitchen, her hands coated in sticky white icing. Thank heavens she'd had the foresight to cover her daughter's clothes with an apron, she thought ruefully. She'd forgotten that she had left Holly stirring the icing while she dealt with the estate agent, and could not blame the little girl for becoming impatient.

'I can see you have, sweetheart,' she murmured, wondering if any icing had actually made it onto the cakes.

Holly stared curiously at Rocco. 'Are you a 'state agent?'

'You mean an *e*state agent,' Emma corrected, but Holly's attention was focused on the big man who dominated the narrow hall. Usually a shy child, she seemed unconcerned by the presence of a stranger in the cottage, and Emma understood why when she glanced back at Rocco and realised with a sinking heart that her little daughter had been charmed by his smile.

'Hello, Holly.' His deep voice was as soft as crushed

velvet. No, I'm not an estate agent. I am your mummy's friend.'

Since when? Emma wanted to demand. But Holly appeared happy with the explanation.

'What's your name?'

'Rocco.'

To Emma's surprise Holly gave Rocco a wide smile. 'Me and Mummy made cupcakes. You can have one if you like.'

The man could charm the birds from the trees—and obviously every female from the age of three to ninety-three, Emma thought irritably, adding the proviso *bar this one*. 'I don't think...Rocco...' she stumbled slightly over his name '...has time at the moment. He was just leaving,' she added pointedly, flicking him a sharp glance.

He returned it with a bland smile and an amused gleam in his eyes before turning his attention back to Holly. 'I would love to try one of your cakes—if Mummy doesn't mind?'

'She doesn't,' Holly assured him innocently. 'I'll get you one.'

'I think we'd better clean you up first,' Emma told her daughter. Determined to take charge of the situation, she pushed open the sitting room door and gave Rocco a cool look that did not disguise her annoyance. 'Perhaps you would like to wait in here?'

'Thank you.' As he stepped past her into the room he briefly brushed against her. The contact was fleeting, yet it sent an electrical current shooting through her body, making her skin tingle as if each of her nerve-endings was acutely sensitive. What would it feel like to be held against his broad chest? To have his arms curve around her and pull her close so that her thighs were pressed against his? Colour surged into Emma's cheeks and she jerked back from him so violently that she hit her head on the door frame.

'Easy,' he murmured gently, as if he were calming a nervous colt. His amber eyes rested speculatively on her flushed face. 'Coffee would be good with a cake—black, no sugar.'

Lord, what she wouldn't give to wipe that arrogant smile from his lips, Emma thought furiously as she stalked into the kitchen. She didn't understand why she was so wound up. Normally she was a calm, even-tempered person, but Rocco D'Angelo got under her skin. She would make him one cup of coffee and then insist that he leave—and too bad if he preferred proper coffee beans, because she only had cheap instant granules.

Holly finished washing her hands at the sink and climbed down from the chair she had been standing on to reach the taps. 'Can I take Rocco a cake now?' At Emma's nod she chose one smothered in icing. 'Rocco's nice,' she stated guilelessly.

Startled, Emma hesitated, torn by the need to gently introduce the notion of 'stranger danger' and at the same time not wanting to alarm her daughter. 'I'm sure he is, but you don't really know him,' she said carefully.

'He's got a nice smile.'

Holly raced out of the kitchen clutching the cake, and for a second Emma felt like rushing after her and snatching the little girl into her arms. *Don't*, she wanted to cry. *Don't be taken in by a charming smile or, when you're older, give your trusting heart to a man who can glibly say the words* I love you *without meaning it.* Smiles were easy and words were cheap—and Jack had had an abundance of both, she thought heavily.

It wasn't Rocco's fault that he reminded her so much of her husband. Not in appearance—Rocco's dark, devilish good-looks were a stark contrast to Jack's blond hair and disarming grin. But, like Rocco, Jack had been supremely self-confident and aware of his effect on the opposite sex. 'A babe-magnet'—that was how her brother had once scathingly described Jack, Emma recalled wryly. From all she knew about Rocco, he was no different. But how could she tell her three-year-old daughter that her mistrust of all men stemmed from the fact that Holly's father had been a deceitful cheat who had broken her heart?

In the sitting room, Rocco strolled over to the fireplace to study the collection of framed photographs displayed on the mantelpiece. The central picture was of a fair-haired man dressed in a fire officer's uniform whom he guessed was Emma's husband. Next to the photo was a silver medal displayed on a velvet cushion. There were several other pictures, including one of Holly as a baby held in her mother's arms, and a recent photo of the little girl standing in front of a Christmas tree in Primrose Cottage. Curiously there were no pictures of Emma with her husband, nor one of him with Holly.

Rocco focused on the photo of the late Jack Marchant. The guy had been undeniably good-looking, with overlong blond hair and brilliant blue eyes, but there was a cockiness about his smile that suggested he had been fully aware of his appeal to women. He would lay a bet that Marchant had been a womaniser before his marriage, Rocco brooded. He had deduced from his own observations the previous evening, and from conversation with his grandmother, that Emma was a rather serious, unassuming person, with a highly developed sense of responsibility. Brash-looking Jack Marchant seemed an unexpected choice of partner for her, but presumably the fact that she still wore her wedding ring three years after being widowed meant that the marriage had been happy and she had loved her husband.

Why did the thought rankle? Rocco wondered irritably, raking a hand through his hair. He didn't know what he was doing here, and if he had any sense he would leave immediately. Only the fact that he had been asked to give a message to Emma from his grandmother prevented him from letting himself out of the front door. But, as his eyes strayed to the photo of the young woman with red-gold hair and a shy smile who was clutching her baby in her arms, he knew he was not being completely honest with himself.

'My daddy was a hero.'

He glanced down to find that Holly had entered the room silently and was standing beside him. She was a pretty child, with hair a shade fairer than her mother's and the same dark grey eyes.

'That's his medal,' she explained, pointing towards the mantelpiece. 'He saved people from a fire. Didn't he, Mummy?' Holly turned to Emma, who had followed her into the room, for confirmation. 'But I never saw him because I was in Mummy's tummy,' she added, her little face becoming solemn for a moment.

'Jack died two months before Holly was born,' Emma told Rocco, seeing the puzzled look in his eyes. 'He rescued three children from a house fire, but was killed when the roof collapsed and he was trapped in the blaze. He was posthumously awarded the Queens Gallantry Medal.'

So her husband had been Superman. Rocco felt a flare of guilt for his uninformed and, as it turned out, unfair assessment of Jack Marchant. For some reason he could not bring himself to look at Emma, and instead smiled at Holly. 'Your *papa* was a brave man. You must be very proud of him.'

He was rewarded with a beaming grin as Holly offered him a sickly looking cake.

'I chose you one with lots of icing.'

Rocco disliked sweet foods, but there was no question of disappointing the child. He bit into the cake. 'Delicious,' he assured Holly, who was watching him anxiously.

She was apparently satisfied with his verdict. 'You'd better finish it before you drop crumbs on the carpet,' she advised him seriously.

'Did you say no sugar in your coffee?' Emma murmured.

Rocco caught the glimmer of amusement in her eyes and gave her a wry look. To his surprise her mouth curved into faint smile, and he felt something kick in his gut. His initial impression of her had been that she was averagely attractive, but he had spent a restless night wondering why he could not dismiss her from his mind and now he realised that she possessed an understated beauty that drew his eyes to her again and again.

'Grazie.' He took the mug of coffee she offered him, his keen gaze noting that her hand shook very slightly. It gave him a measure of satisfaction to see that she was not as composed as she would like him to believe. 'The cake has reminded me of why I'm here,' he murmured. 'I am taking Cordelia to have tea at the Royal Oak Hotel this afternoon, and we would both be delighted if you and Holly would join us.'

'Oh, no—that's very kind, but I don't think so.' Emma's response was immediate, and edged with a flare of panic she could not completely disguise. Spending an afternoon in the company of a devastatingly attractive Italian playboy was not her idea of fun—especially when she was not at all confident she would be able to hide her intense awareness of him. 'I…I have other plans, and I'm sure Cordelia would prefer to have you to herself—especially as she hasn't seen you for so long.'

Rocco chose to ignore the last barbed comment. 'My grandmother issued the invitation. She would very much like you to come.' He paused, his sensual mouth curving at the corners. 'And I am under strict instructions not to take no for an answer.' His smile held genuine warmth and a trace of amusement, as if he knew the reason for her refusal. 'I understand that the hotel has a collection of dolls' houses which children are permitted to play with. Do you like dolls' houses, Holly?' He turned his attention to the little girl, who had been listening to the conversation.

'That's unfair,' Emma muttered, in a voice meant for his ears only, as her daughter nodded enthusiastically.

'Unfair to want to give an elderly lady an enjoyable afternoon?' he countered quietly. 'Cordelia is excited about a trip out, and she is obviously very fond of Holly. Could you not postpone the plans you mentioned until tomorrow?'

He could not possibly know that her plans for the day amounted to watching a new children's DVD with Holly and then attacking the ironing pile.

'Can we have tea with Nonna? Please, Mummy?'

Faced with her daughter's hopeful expression, Emma stifled a sigh of resignation. Holly deserved a treat, and the Royal Oak was renowned for providing excellent play facilities for children and as well as superb food for adults.

She caught Rocco's surprised look and explained, 'Your grandmother suggested that Holly should call her Nonna because she found Cordelia difficult to say.'

It had been touching to witness the special friendship that had developed between her daughter and the elderly lady that was untroubled by the eighty year age gap between them. She forced herself to hold Rocco's gaze, silently cursing the way her heart skittered as she absorbed the masculine beauty of his chiselled features.

'Please tell Cordelia that we would love to accept her invitation.'

'I'll pick you up at three-thirty.'

'There's no need. I'll take my car and meet you at the hotel,' she said quickly. 'I assume your car wasn't seriously damaged last night?' Even if it was in perfect order she had no intention of allowing Holly to travel in a sports car on icy roads.

'Unfortunately the exhaust pipe was ripped from the chassis.' Rocco grimaced when he thought of the several thousand pounds' worth of damage that had been wrought to his Eleganza Classic. He could easily afford the repair bill, but the Classic had been one of the first cars produced by the company his grandfather had established fifty years ago. It was a personal favourite from his private collection of luxury cars—an exquisite piece of engineering which Rocco had lovingly restored. 'Specialist parts will have to be sent over from Italy for it to be repaired, but in the meantime I've hired a car better suited to the wintry conditions,' he explained, nodding towards the window.

Following his gaze, Emma saw a top-of-the-range four-by-four parked outside the cottage, its gleaming paintwork making her battered old vehicle look very much the poor cousin. What it was to have money, she thought wryly. Rocco was a multi-millionaire who lived a jet-setter's glamorous lifestyle very different from her life as a single mother in a quiet Northumberland village. But what did it matter? Soon he would return to Italy, and she would probably never see him again. Surely she could survive one afternoon in his company without making a fool of herself.

'We'll see you at three-thirty then,' she murmured, disguising her anxiety with a cool smile.

* * *

Holly was full of excitement at the prospect of having tea with Nonna and Rocco, and insisted on wearing her best dress that had been a Christmas present.

'Goodness, you've grown,' Emma said ruefully as she surveyed her daughter's skinny legs, where the hem of the dress stopped above her knees. 'Upwards, anyway—I wish you would grow outwards.' The flu virus had left Holly painfully thin and pale. If only she *could* afford a holiday abroad, Emma thought, recalling her conversation with the childminder, Karen. But it was out of the question now that she had to find somewhere else to live.

Determined not to make a big deal out of spending the afternoon with Rocco, she decided to wear her jeans. But at the last minute she changed into the beautiful heather-coloured cashmere jumper her mother had sent for Christmas and teamed it with a fitted grey skirt, sheer hose and her only pair of high-heeled shoes. The Royal Oak Hotel was an upmarket place, and if she was honest it was nice to have a reason to dress up, she admitted, slipping on her grey wool coat as the doorbell rang.

'We're ready,' Holly informed Rocco with a wide grin when Emma opened the door. 'I'm wearing my party dress.' She twirled around to show off her dress, clearly hoping for Rocco's approval.

Once again Emma was surprised by her daughter's eagerness to be friends with him. Holly had never known her father, and although both her grandfathers were alive she only saw them occasionally. Did her daughter wish she had a father, like her best friends the twins, Lily and Sara, had? she wondered. The thought had not occurred to her before, and it troubled her. She did her best to fulfil the role of two parents, but maybe it wasn't enough.

'You look very pretty,' Rocco assured Holly with a soft smile.

Emma was grateful for his gentle patience, which was all the more surprising when he presumably did not come into contact with small children very often, but her heart gave an annoying lurch when he turned his amber eyes on her.

'Both of you,' he murmured.

When they walked down the path she saw that Cordelia was sitting in the back of the car. Beside her was a child's booster seat. 'Up you come,' Rocco said, lifting Holly into the seat and securing the straps. 'You can sit in the front,' he told Emma.

She would rather have sat in the back than next to him, but she could not say so without revealing that he unnerved her and so slid into the front passenger seat without a word. Fortunately Holly chattered non-stop to Cordelia for the entire journey to the hotel, so Emma did not have to make conversation, but she was supremely conscious of Rocco, and could not prevent her eyes from straying to him. He was still wearing the black leather jacket, but had exchanged the jeans and sweater for tailored black trousers and a black shirt, and he looked so devastatingly good-looking that she felt a dull ache of longing in the pit of her stomach.

His hands on the steering wheel were a dark olive colour, and she wondered if the rest of his body was as tanned. A series of erotic images filled her mind and she quickly turned her head and stared out of the window, her cheeks burning. It was going to be a long afternoon, she thought ruefully, and the most annoying thing was that her tension was self-inflicted. She did not *want* to feel this fierce attraction to Cordelia's playboy grandson, but she did not seem to have a choice.

* * *

It was almost six o'clock when they returned to Primrose Cottage.

'Thank you for a lovely afternoon.' Emma's smile briefly encompassed Rocco, before she turned her head to Cordelia in the back of the car. 'Holly had a wonderful time. I'm not surprised she's fallen asleep. I've never known her to talk so much.'

Despite her reservations, the afternoon had been enjoyable. Holly had been in heaven playing with the dolls' houses in the charming family room of the hotel, where tea—comprising an extensive selection of sandwiches and cakes—had been served. Kept busy trying to persuade Holly to eat, and chatting to Cordelia, Emma had been distracted from her intense awareness of Rocco, and apart from a conversation when she had asked about his company and he had given her a brief history of Eleganza, there had been little verbal contact between them.

There had been eye contact, though, she remembered. Throughout the afternoon she had been conscious of his gaze resting on her, and on several occasions she had darted him a quick glance and blushed when her eyes had collided with his. His expression had been speculative, and when she had walked back to the table after playing with Holly he had subjected her to a bold appraisal which had made her breasts feel heavy and caused her nipples to harden into tight buds which mercifully could not be seen through her woollen jumper.

The memory of the predatory gleam in his amber gaze made her feel edgy, and she quickly released her seat belt and opened the car door.

'There's no need for you to get out,' she told him. 'You should take Cordelia home before she gets cold.'

'I'll leave the engine and the heater running while I carry Holly inside,' he replied equably. 'Go and open the front door, Emma,' he bade her, in a tone that brooked no argument when she opened her mouth to do just that.

Irritating man, she thought as she marched up the front path and fitted her key in the lock. She had cared for Holly on her own for three years and she did not need his help. She glanced over her shoulder and saw that Holly had half woken, but instead of being alarmed to find herself in Rocco's arms the little girl contentedly rested her head on his shoulder.

She didn't feel *jealous*, Emma reassured herself. But it was hard to watch her daughter instinctively snuggle up to Rocco, as if he had already become a part of their lives. He wasn't—and never would be. She certainly did not want Holly to become attached to him only to be upset when he returned to Italy.

She watched him carefully deposit the sleepy child on the sofa in the sitting room, and then followed him back into the hall. 'Thank you again for a pleasant afternoon.' She flushed, realising how stilted she sounded. 'Holly... *we*,' she corrected, 'really enjoyed it.'

'I'm glad you did not find an afternoon in my company *too* much of an ordeal,' Rocco murmured dryly.

In the narrow hallway he was too close for comfort: six feet plus of big, dark, broad-shouldered male towering over her, emphasising the fact that she was slightly below average height. Emma closed her eyes in a vain attempt to lessen her awareness of him, but her other senses immediately became more acute, so that the scent of his aftershave and the warmth emanating from his body stole around her.

Her lashes flew open when she felt something brush her cheek, her eyes widening in shock when he gently tucked a strand of her hair behind her ear. The gesture was unacceptable from a man she barely knew. It was an intrusion on her personal space and she knew she should tell him to back off. Yet the feather-light touch of his fingertips against her skin was beguiling. It was so long since she had been touched by a man.

Since she had discovered the truth about Jack's infidelity—or rather infidelities, she thought bleakly—she had built a defensive wall around her emotions. Was she going to allow that wall to be breached by a notorious playboy— a man who, if the reports she had heard about him were true, was even more unreliable than her husband?

The vulnerability in Emma's storm-cloud-grey eyes took Rocco by surprise. His instincts told him that someone had hurt her in the past—what other reason could there be for her to shy away from him like a nervous colt whenever he came within a foot of her? But who had made her so defensive? He thought of the photograph on the mantelpiece of swaggering Jack Marchant, and his eyes strayed to her wedding ring, remembering how often she had unconsciously twisted it on her finger during the afternoon.

She must have loved her husband to still be wearing his ring three years after his death. But if not Marchant who was responsible for the haunted expression in her eyes? And why did he care? he asked himself irritably. For reasons he was damned if he could explain, he found himself wanting to slide his fingers into her shiny bell of hair and draw her close. Only the slight tremor of her lower lip held him back from dipping his head and slanting his mouth over hers. She intrigued and infuriated him in equal measure: one minute a brisk, ultra-efficient nurse, the next a sensual woman whose wary expression could not disguise her sexual awareness of him.

She stepped away from him and pulled open the front door. 'Goodnight.'

He detected the faint note of desperation in her voice

and took pity on her. *'Ciao, bella,'* he drawled softly, his eyes lingering on her flushed face before he turned and strode down the path.

CHAPTER FOUR

So he had called her beautiful! It meant nothing, Emma told herself impatiently. A man like Rocco probably called all his women *bella*, so that he did not have to bother remembering their names.

Not that *she* was one of his women, her brain pointed out, nor was she ever likely to be. She did not need a man in her life—certainly not a gorgeous, sexy Italian who changed his mistresses more often than most men changed their socks.

A faint smell of burning dragged her from her thoughts and she cursed as she lifted the iron and saw the singe marks on her new white blouse. This was ridiculous. For the sake of her sanity, not to mention the pile of clothes still waiting to be ironed, she *had* to put Rocco out of her mind. He had disrupted her day, but she was not going to allow him to disrupt her life.

After he had left to drive Cordelia home to Nunstead Hall, Emma had carried Holly upstairs to bed. For the second night in a row the little girl had been too weary for a bath and had fallen back to sleep within minutes of her head touching the pillow. As she'd watched Holly's long eyelashes settle on her pale cheeks Emma's heart had clenched with love. Her precious daughter was the centre of her life and there was no room for anyone else. How could there be after Jack? she thought bitterly.

The discovery of his betrayal had shattered all her illusions about love and trust, but he had died before she could confront him. She would never know if he had planned to stay and be a father to Holly, or walk out on his marriage and his child as his mistress had insisted had been his intention.

But, whatever Jack might have planned, fate had intervened, and Emma had given birth to her daughter alone. From the start of Holly's life it had been just the two of them. And that suited her fine, Emma reminded herself. She loved being a mother, she enjoyed a rewarding career and she had good friends and a supportive family. She was content with all that she had. So why tonight did she feel that something was missing?

The ironing had lost its limited appeal, and she stacked the board and the laundry basket in the utility room, promising herself she would finish it tomorrow. On Saturday nights after Holly was in bed she usually curled up on the sofa to watch a DVD and treated herself to a bar of chocolate. She duly slid a film into the player and settled down to watch it, determinedly ignoring the voice in her head that whispered insidiously that she was lonely.

The peal of the doorbell caused her to tense. Was it a sixth sense that warned the unexpected visitor was Rocco—or wishful thinking? But why would he have driven all the way back from Nunstead Hall through the sleety rain that had replaced yesterday's snowfall? Common sense told her to slide the security chain across before she opened the door, and her heart flipped at the sight of her nemesis leaning nonchalantly against the porch, looking devastatingly sexy with the collar of his leather jacket pulled up around his face and a lock of black hair falling across his brow.

He took her breath away. She did not trust herself to speak and instead arched her brows in silent query.

'I thought tonight would be a good time to discuss my grandmother's living arrangements,' he greeted her. His lazy smile did strange things to her insides. 'And to share this excellent Pinot Noir,' he added, holding out a bottle of red wine.

Emma shook her head. 'Not now—it's late—'

'It's half past eight on a Saturday evening,' he interrupted her. 'Admittedly Cordelia was going to bed when I left, but she's eighty-three.'

The amusement in his voice made her blush. 'Well, maybe I'm busy,' she said tightly. 'Or maybe I would prefer not to spend my leisure time dealing with work issues— had that occurred to you?'

'I didn't realise you considered Cordelia's welfare to be a work issue.' His voice hardened. 'I believed you thought of her as a friend.'

'I do—of course I do.' She flushed uncomfortably. For weeks she had wanted to discuss her concerns about her patient with Cordelia's grandson. Now Rocco was here to do just that, and innate honesty forced her to admit that she had no good reason not to invite him in. Apart from the fact that he made her feel as edgy and awkward as a teenager with a severe crush on him, she acknowledged silently.

The thought had suddenly occurred to Rocco that perhaps Emma's reluctance to invite him in was because she already had a visitor—a male visitor. He frowned, startled by how strongly he disliked the idea.

'If you're entertaining, then I apologise for interrupting your evening,' he said stiffly.

Emma blinked in surprise. Did he think she spent her Saturday nights partying? *He* might lead a jet-set lifestyle, but her social life consisted of attending the monthly meeting of the village council in the church hall.

'Who on earth do you think I would be *entertaining* on a night like this?'

The temperature must be hovering just above freezing, because rain rather than snow was still falling. She suddenly realised that the porch offered him little protection from the weather. 'Just a minute.' She closed the door, released the security chain, and then opened it again, moving back so that he could step inside.

He smelled of rain and leather—and the musky scent of his aftershave that was already tantalisingly familiar to her. In the narrow hall she was immediately conscious of his size, and his raw masculinity seemed like an alien invasion of her cosy cottage with its pastel-coloured, feminine décor.

'Please come on through,' she mumbled, trying to ignore the erratic thud of her heart as she led the way into the sitting room.

'I thought you might have a boyfriend here.' He returned to the conversation he had begun on the doorstep. The gleam in his eyes was faintly challenging and openly curious.

Emma met his gaze levelly. 'I don't have a boyfriend,' she revealed, in a cool tone intended to deter further discussion on the subject.

Rocco did not seem to get the message. 'I guess it must be difficult to meet other men and pursue a relationship when you have a young child?'

She shrugged. 'I'm not interested in meeting men, so I wouldn't know.'

His eyes narrowed on her stony face. 'But you must

date occasionally. Your husband has been dead how long? Three years?'

'I really don't think my private life is any of your business.' She should have followed her first instinct and slammed the front door on him, she thought angrily, her tension mounting when he strolled across the room and studied the photographs on the mantelpiece.

'You don't date other men three years after your husband's death, yet you don't have any pictures of the two of you on display—not even a wedding photo,' he murmured. 'Why not?'

'I find it too painful to look at pictures of my wedding day.'

She had given the same excuse to Jack's parents, and it was the truth—although not for the reasons they believed. She could not bear to see the photos of herself smiling adoringly at the man she had loved, and Jack smiling adoringly at the camera.

He had been well aware that his blond good-looks made him extremely photogenic, and had loved being the centre of attention—unlike the bride, Emma thought ruefully. Never one to seek the spotlight, she had found their big white wedding an ordeal. But Jack had wanted it, and she had been so madly in love with him, and so amazed that he had chosen her for his wife when he could have had any woman he desired, that she would have flown to the moon to marry him if he had suggested it.

What a blind fool she had been. Her wedding photos were a painful reminder of her gullibility, for she had trusted Jack and believed him when he had told her she was the only woman he would ever want. But by the time she had discovered that he had had numerous affairs throughout the three years of their marriage he had been dead.

For the sake of his distraught parents she had kept the

truth to herself. Jack had died a hero, and it would have been cruel to taint Peter and Alison's image of their only son by revealing that he had been a lying cheat. She had struggled alone to come to terms with the two very different sides of her husband—one so admirable, and the other causing her so much heartache. She knew her parents had their suspicions that her marriage had not been as rosy as she pretended, but she had not even confided in them. Holly believed that the father who had died before she was born was a wonderful heroic figure, and Emma did not want anyone to shatter her daughter's illusion.

Rocco was watching her with a speculative look in his eyes that she found unnerving. 'I'm not in the mood to play a game of twenty questions,' she snapped. 'I thought the reason for your visit was to discuss what to do about your grandmother?'

'It is—and on that subject I have a suggestion to put to you.' Rocco stifled his impatience to learn more about Emma's relationship with her husband. He was good at reading body language, and her obvious tension when he had mentioned Jack Marchant fired his curiosity. But he could see she was regretting inviting him in. If she asked him to leave he would have no option but to comply, and so he masked his frustration with a smile.

Besides, the main purpose of his visit *was* with regard to Cordelia, he reminded himself. During tea at the hotel this afternoon he had witnessed the genuine friendship between his grandmother and Emma. Her kindness and compassion were traits distinctly lacking in the brittle socialites he usually associated with, and he readily admitted that he was impressed by her caring nature. His unexpected attraction to her was *not* the reason why he was here.

He waved the bottle of wine he was holding. 'Do you have a corkscrew? We'll have a drink while we talk.'

'There's one in the kitchen.' Emma took the wine bottle from him, wishing she had the nerve to tell him she had changed her mind and wanted him to go. Good manners insisted she play the role of hostess. 'Would you like me to take your jacket?'

'*Grazie.*' He shrugged out of the leather jacket and handed it to her.

The lining was still warm from his body. It seemed strangely intimate to hold something that seconds ago had sheathed his muscular torso. What would it feel like to be held against that broad chest, to press her cheek to his silk shirt and feel his arms close around her?

The image evoked a wistful pang of longing to feel protected, cherished. Her friends and family often commented on how well she coped as a single mother. She defined herself as being quietly confident, capable and independent. So why did the idea of being held safe in a pair of strong arms suddenly seem so enticing? And who was she kidding? she thought impatiently, as she walked out to the hall and hung Rocco's jacket over the stair banister. *Safe* was not a word she would equate with Rocco D'Angelo.

The corkscrew was hiding at the back of the cutlery drawer, which went to show how infrequently she drank wine. She was struggling to remove the cork from the bottle when he strolled into the kitchen.

'Allow me to do that.'

Rocco uncorked the wine with practised ease and watched Emma open a cupboard and retrieve two glasses. She had to stretch up to reach them, and in doing so her fine wool sweater was drawn taut across her breasts, emphasising their rounded fullness. Heat flared in his groin, prompting him to shift his position to ease the constriction of his suddenly tight trousers. The kitchen was built to the same minuscule proportions as the rest of the cottage. One step was all it would take to bring his body into contact with Emma's. But he fought the temptation to press himself against her soft curves and glanced around the room, feeling the top of his head brush against the ceiling beams.

'I hope the agent deters anyone tall from viewing this place. It's not much bigger than a dolls' house.'

'It's big enough for the two of us,' Emma said shortly, her heart sinking at the reminder that she would soon be forced to move out of the cottage which had been her home for the past three years.

'Did you live here when your husband was alive?'

'No—Jack was based at a fire station in the centre of Newcastle, and we lived in a flat nearby. I moved to Primrose Cottage after Holly was born.'

'What made you come out here to this isolated village? I would have thought Little Copton was too quiet for a young woman. It must be difficult to have a social life when you're so far from a decent sized town.'

'I don't want a social life—not in the way you mean… visiting nightclubs and bars,' Emma added, flushing when Rocco gave her a quizzical look. 'I did part of my nurse's training at Hexham Hospital, and used to spend my days off exploring the moors. My parents wanted me to move back to their farm in Scotland with Holly, but when I saw Primrose Cottage I fell in love with it.'

She knew her parents had been worried about her living on her own with a newborn baby, but she had craved isolation, wanting to be alone to grieve for Jack and come to terms with the knowledge that he hadn't loved her as she had loved him. The discovery of how he had betrayed her had decimated her sense of self-worth, and like a wounded animal she had gone to ground.

Three years on she was proud of the fact that she was in control of her life, and utterly determined never to relinquish her independence or risk her emotional stability. It would be easy to be dazzled by a man like Rocco, she brooded. The way her heart skittered at his sexy smile was annoying proof that she was not completely immune to his charisma. But she had fallen for a charmer once before and been bitterly hurt. She wasn't stupid enough to do so again.

Rocco skimmed his eyes over Emma's silky bob of hair and her creamy skin, noting the faint dusting of red-gold freckles on her nose and cheeks. 'So you're Scottish—I thought I detected an accent.'

She shook her head. 'Not technically—my family moved to Scotland from London when I was ten, so my Scots burr is not as strong as if I'd been born north of the border.'

'Are they your parents?' Rocco indicated the photo on the dresser of Holly with an older man and woman.

'My in-laws. They adore Holly.' Emma studied the picture of Jack's parents and saw the sadness in the eyes that their smiles could not disguise. They had been devastated by the loss of their son, and doted on their little granddaughter. For them and for Holly she would continue with the pretence that Jack had been a devoted husband, and never reveal that he had shattered her trust irrevocably.

She had joined Rocco by the dresser when he had asked about the photo, and now she was acutely conscious of how close they were standing. The fine hairs on her body stood on end, each of her senses alerted to his sheer maleness as she inhaled the subtle musk of aftershave and pheromones.

Why did he affect her so strongly? she wondered despairingly. And how had he drawn so much personal information from her without her even realising it. So much for keeping him at a distance!

She forced a cool smile. 'We seem to have diverted from

the subject of Cordelia. Let's go back to the other room and you can tell me about your plans for how best to care for her.'

She preceded him into the sitting room and offered him the sofa, but instead of sitting next to him she crossed to the armchair on the other side of the room.

He poured the wine and handed her a glass. 'Wouldn't you be more comfortable over here? Where you can put your drink on the coffee table?'

She felt herself blush at the amused gleam in his eyes. 'I'm fine where I am, thank you.' Determined not to show how much he rattled her, she settled back in the chair and took a long sip of wine. It was deliciously smooth and fruity, and she felt a relaxing warmth seep through her veins. 'So, what do you intend to do about Cordelia? I'm afraid the local health authority won't provide a live-in carer for her, but there are a number of private agencies who could arrange for staff to visit her every day.'

Rocco shook his head. 'I can see that Nonna needs more than that. She's too frail to continue living at Nunstead Hall—even with regular visits from carers. And employing live-in staff has not proved successful.'

'Then what do you propose? Cordelia is adamant that she won't move from Nunstead.'

'I've discovered that,' Rocco said with feeling, recalling his grandmother's stubbornness on the subject. 'As a temporary measure, while she is recovering from the hip operation and the burn to her hand, I've asked her to come and stay with me at my home in Portofino.'

Emma's eyebrows arched in surprise. 'And she's agreed?'

'No—not yet. But I've had an idea that I think will persuade her.' He looked across the room, his tiger-like amber eyes trapping her gaze. 'I've hinted that you might come to Italy to be her private nurse.'

She had been in the process of taking another sip of wine, but at his startling statement the sip became a gulp. The alcohol must have gone straight to her head, because for a second her brain felt fuzzy before his words sank in. 'Well, you'd better *un*-hint,' she said sharply. 'I have no intention of moving to Italy. The idea is ridiculous—and impossible.'

'Why?' Rocco queried calmly. 'I'm not suggesting a permanent arrangement. My suggestion to Cordelia is that she comes to my home for three months' convalescence. After that we will decide whether she is able to return to Nunstead, with the help of a live-in carer, or—as I'm secretly hoping—she will have settled in Italy and will agree to remain living with me. At first she point-blank refused to consider the idea, because she was worried she would be lonely and miss her friends here in Northumberland. But it's clear that *you* are her closest friend, Emma,' he said softly, and the husky way he murmured her name sent an involuntary quiver down Emma's spine. 'When I put forward the idea that you could come to Portofino for three months, Nonna was much happier to consider my plan.'

'You had no right to suggest that to Cordelia without asking me first,' Emma said tightly. What Rocco had done amounted to emotional blackmail, and she was furious with him. 'It doesn't seem to have crossed your mind that I have a life here in England—a job, *a child*. I can't simply take off for three months and abandon my responsibilities, and no way on earth would I ever leave Holly with my parents for that length of time. The most she's ever been away from me is a weekend, when Jack's parents took her to stay at their house in France.'

Rocco's dark brows drew together in a frown, his anger

mounting at her diatribe and the unspoken accusation that *he* had abandoned *his* responsibility for his grandmother over the past months.

'When did I say you would have to leave Holly?' he demanded. 'Naturally you would bring her with you. You say you have a life here that you don't wish to leave, but you're going to have to move out of this cottage. You've already told me there's no man around and you're not involved in a relationship—so what exactly is holding you back from taking a three month sabbatical from your job to help an old lady you insist you care about?'

'Dozens of things,' Emma muttered, infuriated by his casual attitude. 'For a start, I need to look for somewhere to live.'

'That's not a problem. I'll have one of my staff research suitable properties for you, and once you've chosen a place I'll arrange the move.'

He made it sound so simple, she thought irritably. But his wealth inured him to the mundane problems of day-to-day living that most people experienced. She was sure he had never had to worry about how much rent he could afford, or deal with unscrupulous landlords who demanded a huge deposit but failed to carry out vital repairs. She had been lucky that the owner of Primrose Cottage was a decent, kindly man; there was no guarantee that her next tenancy would be as trouble free.

But, as Rocco had pointed out, her life *was* going to change whether she liked it or not, she thought heavily. However, that did not mean that she should uproot her daughter and take her to live temporarily in another country.

'It's important for Holly to feel settled and secure.'

'I'm sure it is, and I am certain she will love my home in Portofino. The Villa Lucia has ten guest bedrooms and there is plenty of space for a child to play inside, or out-side in the four acres of gardens. Already there is plenty of spring sunshine, and in a month the weather will be warm enough for trips to the beach. You were only saying earlier today how you wished you could take Holly for a holiday to help her recuperate from the flu virus that has left her so pale and robbed her of her appetite,' he reminded her.

Emma could not deny she had said exactly that, when Holly had refused to eat more than half a sandwich at the hotel. 'But it won't *be* a holiday,' she pointed out. 'Who will look after Holly while I'm working?'

'It won't be work as such. Cordelia doesn't need nursing. I simply want you to act as a companion to her. And you know as well as I do that she loves having Holly around. I can't see why you have a problem with the idea,' he said, frustration edging into his voice. 'It seems the perfect so-lution—I'll know that my grandmother is safe and happy, and Holly will get to spend three months where the climate is a good deal warmer than in Northumberland.'

When he put it like that it was difficult see a problem with his plan, she admitted. But there *was* a problem—and he was it. Or rather, she had a problem with the idea of living in his home for three months. She could hide her attraction to him while he was staying at Nunstead Hall and she was only likely to meet him occasionally. But to stay with him at his villa and see him every day—that was something else.

She wished he didn't unsettle her. He was offering her a golden opportunity to give Holly a wonderful holiday and she was angry with herself for allowing him to affect her. But he stirred feelings inside her she had been sure she would never feel again—desires that she'd believed had died when she had learned how Jack had betrayed her. Even now her mind was only half concentrated on what he was saying, while the other half was swamped by her intense awareness of his smouldering virility.

'I'm sorry, but my answer is no,' she said stiffly.

'Why not?' Rocco struggled to contain his frustration. It hadn't occurred to him that Emma might refuse. In his position as CEO of Eleganza he was used to people doing his bidding without question, and in his personal life he had never yet failed to charm a woman around to his way of thinking.

'I have my reasons.'

'Which are *what*?' He could not think of one good reason why she would turn down a three month sojourn in a beautiful part of the world, for which she would get paid. 'If it's a question of money, obviously I will pay you the top rate for a live-in nurse. Nonna won't come without you,' he said harshly, glaring at Emma's mutinous expression. 'What am I going to do? We both know it's not safe for her to remain at Nunstead, but I have commitments in Italy that mean I have to return there next week.'

Emma tried to quash her pang of guilt. She could not deny that it would be best for Cordelia to go and stay with Rocco, but he would have to find another way of persuading his grandmother to accompany him to Portofino.

'I'm sorry if you have led Cordelia to think I would go to Italy with her, but I can't. And I don't see why I should have to explain my reasons to you—a man I met for the first time yesterday,' she added fiercely, her temper rising when she saw the angry gleam in his amber eyes. 'That's all I have to say on the subject.' She jumped to her feet. 'I think you should leave.'

She was throwing him out! No woman had ever asked Rocco to leave, and the novel experience was not one he relished. But he had stated his case—or rather his grandmother's case—and he was damned if he was going to plead with Emma to reconsider, he thought grimly. Without another word he stood up, and placed his glass on the coffee table at the same time as Emma set down her half-full glass. Their fingers brushed and she snatched her hand away, sending the glass flying so that red wine cascaded across the table and dripped over the edge.

'*Blast!*' She stared in horror at the spreading stain on the cream carpet. 'It had to happen now. The estate agent phoned earlier to say he's arranged for someone to view the cottage tomorrow.'

'I'll get a cloth.' Rocco was already striding from the room.

Emma hurried along to the kitchen after him, and while he grabbed the dishcloth she rummaged in a cupboard, looking for the carpet cleaning solution she was sure was stashed at the back—before remembering she had used the last of it to clean up a spill at Christmas.

'Is the stain very bad? I've brought another cloth.' She ran back into the sitting room just as he was emerging, and they collided in the doorway.

'It's fine. I've cleaned it up and you can't see a mark, so stop flapping.'

His impatient tone brought her up sharp. 'I never *flap*,' she said tightly, flushing as she realised she had been doing just that.

What the hell was wrong with her? she asked herself furiously. She had spent two years working in an A&E unit, often dealing with life-threatening emergencies, yet here she was getting in a stew about spilt wine.

Rocco set her nerves on edge, she acknowledged ruefully. Ever since she had invited him into the cottage she had been conscious of the undercurrent of sexual awareness. And now they were jammed in the doorway, with their bodies touching, and molten heat was coursing through her veins.

Her eyes were drawn against her will to his face, and her heart gave a violent thud when she watched his gaze narrow and become predatory. Time stood still and the air between them quivered. He stared down at her, as if he could see deep into her soul, before he slowly lowered his head.

He was going to kiss her. She knew she should move, break the spell he had cast on her, but it was too late. His warm breath whispered across her lips and involuntarily she parted them as he claimed her mouth. With practised ease he took possession of her, sliding a hand to her nape as he deepened the kiss, yet keeping the caress non-threatening, so that she slowly relaxed and allowed her body to settle against him while she responded to the gentle demands of his mouth.

She was drowning in a sea of sensation. There was nothing but Rocco's strong, hard body pressing against her, so that she could feel his powerful thigh muscles through her skirt. His hand slid from her nape to tangle in her hair, holding her still while he subtly increased the pressure of his lips on hers and took the kiss to another level that was blatantly erotic.

Without conscious thought she lifted her arms to his shoulders, a tremor running through her when he curled his arm around her waist and drew her even closer, so that she could feel the thud of his heart and, more enticingly, the solid ridge of his arousal straining beneath his trousers.

He delicately probed between her lips with his tongue before initiating a bold exploration that made her tremble. Reality had ceased to exist. All she was aware of was the faint abrasion of his jaw against her cheek and the softness of his hair as she curved her arms around his neck and slid her fingers into the dark mass of silk above his collar.

At first slow and sweet, the tenure of his kiss changed to hot and hungry, seducing her with its innate sensuality. Nothing had prepared her for the wild, almost primitive pleasure he evoked, and she responded with a feverish urgency as her defences crumbled.

From upstairs came the sound of Holly coughing. The sexually charged silence down in the hall immediately shattered, and Emma dragged her mouth from Rocco's, her chest heaving as she snatched oxygen into her lungs. Dear heaven, what if her daughter had got out of bed and discovered her kissing a virtual stranger? What if Holly hadn't coughed and she had continued to kiss Rocco with the wanton abandon that had overwhelmed her mere seconds ago?

'What are you doing?' she demanded shakily.

His dark brows rose quizzically. 'What am *I* doing? Surely you mean what are *we* doing? And I think the answer is pretty self-explanatory,' he drawled softly. He trailed a lazy hand down to her breast and brushed across the hard peak of her nipple jutting beneath her jumper.

'Don't!' Mortified by her response to him, she snatched her arms from around his neck and sidestepped him out of the doorway into the hall, struggling to control her erratic breathing. 'You took me by surprise.' Panic made her voice sharp as she felt a growing sense of horror at her behaviour. 'You had no right to come on to me.'

Rocco raked a hand through his hair, surprised by the strength of his desire for Emma, and his fierce urge to pull her back into his arms and kiss her into submission. 'It was just a kiss.' He managed to sound coolly dismissive, even though his heart was pounding in his chest. 'There's no need to get worked up about it.'

He sounded faintly bored, as if he was used to kissing women he barely knew on a passing whim—which he probably was, she conceded sickly. No doubt he had confidently expected her to invite him up to her bedroom, or maybe he would have led her back into the sitting room and removed her clothes—*his*—before making love to her on the sofa? Her face burned as erotic images of their naked, entwined limbs flooded her mind.

'You shouldn't have done it.' Her voice sounded thick, almost guttural, as she fought the shockingly fierce pull of sexual desire that throbbed low in her pelvis. 'I told you, I'm not looking for a...' She faltered on the word *relationship*, certain that Rocco wanted nothing more than casual sex. 'I don't want a man in my life.'

As she looked through the doorway into the sitting room, the photograph of Jack's grinning face seemed to mock her. Rocco followed her gaze and his face hardened.

'He's been dead for three years. He might have been a hero, but you can't grieve for him for ever,' he said harshly. His eyes narrowed on her face as a startling realisation dawned. 'You're not telling me I'm the first man you've kissed since you were widowed?'

'I'm not telling you anything.' Her marriage was not open to discussion. Holly coughed again. 'Our voices are disturbing her,' she muttered, glancing towards the stairs. The maternal instinct to go and check on her daughter finally released her from Rocco's magnetic spell. *'Please go.'*

Arguing with her was not going to get him anywhere, Rocco realised frustratedly as he snatched up his jacket and yanked open the front door. And, when it came down to it, what *did* he actually want? He hadn't meant for things to get so out of hand. Hell, he hadn't meant to kiss her. But when he had stared into her soft grey eyes he had felt compelled by a force he'd had no control over to slant his mouth over hers.

The uncomfortable throb of his erection was a mocking reminder that Emma turned him on more than any woman had done for a long time. But it was patently obvious that she was still in love with her dead husband—and, although Rocco eschewed any degree of emotional attachment with his mistresses, he balked at the idea of making love to a woman who wished he was someone else.

CHAPTER FIVE

THE weather on Sunday mimicked Emma's mood: grey, gloomy and unsettled. Holly refused to eat breakfast or lunch, and the cough that had developed during the night racked her fragile frame.

'When will the sun come out?' She sighed, her nose pressed to the window as she watched the rain falling relentlessly from a leaden sky. 'I want to play in the garden.'

'Spring will soon be here,' Emma promised. But she was assailed by guilt when she recalled Rocco's suggestion that she should accompany Cordelia to his home in Portofino and give her daughter a three-month holiday in the Italian sunshine. It was out of the question now, she thought grimly. She had proved last night that she could not trust herself to resist her sexual attraction to him.

She determinedly pushed him to the back of her mind and concentrated on finishing the household chores so that she could play with Holly, eventually slotting a favourite DVD into the player when it became clear that the little girl was weary.

During the afternoon, a retired couple came to view the cottage, and enthused over its quaint charm. A phone call from her landlord a few hours later, to inform her that the couple had offered the full asking price and were eager for the sale to go through quickly, rounded off a bad day and preceded a second restless night when Rocco invaded her thoughts until the early hours.

On Monday Holly woke with a high temperature which, together with her worsening cough, warranted a trip to the doctor. He diagnosed a chest infection.

'I wish I could prescribe fresh air and a dose of sunshine rather than antibiotics,' he said ruefully.

Luckily Emma managed to reschedule most of her day's visits, and a colleague agreed to cover her more serious cases. 'It's just Mrs Symmonds that I'll have trouble fitting in,' Sandra explained. 'She lives so far out on the moors.'

'I'll go and see her, and take Holly with me.' She had to face Rocco some time, so she might as well get it over with, Emma brooded as the four-by-four splashed through deep puddles made by the rain and melting snow on the road leading to Nunstead Hall.

Her knock on the door brought no response. Assuming that Rocco was busy somewhere in the huge house, she used the key Cordelia had given her. But as she stepped into the hall she immediately realised that for some reason the central heating wasn't on. It was almost as cold inside as out in the bitter wind blowing across the moors.

Cordelia was in the living room, sitting in an armchair pulled up close to the fire that was smouldering in the grate. She looked unusually pale, and her eyes were closed. For a second Emma's heart stopped, and she drew a relieved breath when the elderly lady stirred.

'Why is the heating off—?' She broke off and stared at Cordelia's hands—one bandaged to cover her burn, the other purple and bruised, with the fingers swollen to twice their normal size. 'What on earth has happened to your hand?'

'I opened the back door to call Thomas, and a gust of wind blew it shut and trapped my fingers,' Cordelia explained in a shaky voice. 'Rocco doesn't think they're broken because I can move them.' She winced as she wiggled her bruised fingers a fraction.

'They must be agony.' Emma felt physically sick as she inspected the elderly lady's injured fingers. Desperately worried about her patient, she repeated her first question. 'Why is the house so cold?'

'The heating has broken down. Something to do with the boiler, I think Rocco said.' As she finished speaking, Cordelia closed her eyes once more. She looked heart-wrenchingly fragile, and was probably suffering from mild shock, Emma realised.

'Where *is* Rocco?'

'Oh, he went to Paris to meet one of his lady friends… today…or was it yesterday?' Cordelia shook her head. 'I'm a bit muddled.' She smiled faintly. 'He's such a Lothario— just like his father.'

For a few seconds Emma was too shocked to speak. 'You mean he's left you injured and alone in a freezing house to go on a *date*?' The sick feeling in the pit of her stomach intensified, and with it a growing sense of outrage that Rocco had so casually abandoned his grandmother. Professionalism held her back from voicing her opinion that he was the most heartless and irresponsible man she had ever met, but she could not dismiss the little voice in her head which taunted that his beautiful mistress Juliette Pascal lived in Paris. Clearly kissing *her* on Saturday night had been an aberration which he had probably already forgotten about, Emma thought grimly.

She needed to focus on her job, she reminded herself. Her priority was to arrange temporary accommodation for Cordelia in a nursing home, where she could be properly cared for. Stubborn as the old lady was, she would surely understand that she could not remain on her own at Nunstead Hall.

Emma glanced at Holly, who was coughing again. 'Keep your coat on, munchkin, and stay in here, where it's a bit warmer than the rest of the house. I'm going to go and make Cordelia a cup of tea.'

The little girl nodded and patted Cordelia gently. 'I'll look after you, Nonna. Shall I tell you the story about the three little pigs?'

The weariness in Cordelia's eyes faded, and she smiled. 'That would be lovely, darling.'

The special bond between her daughter and her elderly patient was so poignant, Emma brooded as she hurried down to the kitchen. She knew the two of them would enjoy spending time together in Italy, and once again she felt guilty that she had refused to accept the position as Cordelia's private nurse. The truth was she could not bear the idea of staying at Rocco's villa, where he no doubt entertained an ever-changing parade of gorgeous women. It would be torture, she thought dismally. And it would be all the worse because she bitterly resented her attraction to a man she disliked.

She was suddenly jolted from her thoughts when she felt a blast of cold air rush into the kitchen, and as she glanced towards the back door her eyes widened in shock.

'I thought you were in Paris?'

Rocco frowned at the accusatory tone of Emma's voice, but he was intrigued when she blushed and quickly looked away from him. 'I was there yesterday,' he told her with a shrug.

One half of Emma's brain was busy registering that he looked unbelievably gorgeous in faded jeans and the big sheepskin jacket that emphasised the width of his broad shoulders, his damp hair brushed back from his brow to reveal the stark beauty of his features. But the other half of her brain was clinically assessing his words. So it was true—after he had made a pass at her he had gone straight to visit his French mistress. It was utterly ridiculous to feel so betrayed, she told herself fiercely. She was aware of his playboy reputation. And his kiss had meant as little to her as it clearly had to him, she assured herself.

She thought of Jack, who—although she had not known it at the time—had sometimes made love to her only hours after he had spent the afternoon having sex with his mistress. Since his death she had supressed the anger that simmered inside her, but now it rose up in an unstoppable tide. She wanted to lash out at her husband, who had hurt her so badly, but Jack was dead. It was Rocco standing in front of her—Rocco, who for a few breathless moments on Saturday night had made her feel like an attractive woman. For all she knew he might have been thinking about Juliette Pascal while he had been kissing her, she thought sickly.

She launched into a furious attack. 'I can't believe you went to Paris and left Cordelia when you *knew* the central heating was broken, and after she had injured her hand so badly. It was utterly *despicable* of you. Good God— couldn't you have controlled your sexual urges? Or is your grandmother's welfare unimportant compared to you getting it on with Juliette What's-Her-Name?'

For thirty seconds after her tirade silence trembled in the kitchen before Rocco demanded in an icy voice, 'What the hell are you talking about?'

'*You* scurrying off to meet your mistress the day after you had kissed me. That's what I'm talking about.' Emma's voice rose several notches. 'I don't give a damn what you do, or who you do it with,' she assured him scathingly. 'But to leave Cordelia alone in a freezing cold house was unforgivable.'

'I did not leave her on her own.' His tenuous control on his temper exploded. *'Dio*, woman—it's a pity you don't check your facts before making wild and totally unjust accusations.'

'You don't deny that you went to Paris?' Emma snapped.

'No, I don't deny it. But Cordelia spent the whole of Sunday with Jim and Nora Yaxley at their farm. I took her over in the morning, flew to Paris on my private jet, and spent a few hours there before I returned in the evening to collect her. This morning I woke to find that the central heating had packed up,' he explained curtly. 'I called an engineer, and while I was showing him the boiler Cordelia injured her hand in the door. I checked to make sure she hadn't broken any bones, and then lit a fire in the sitting room to keep her warm while I went to chop some logs.' He glared at her coldly, with no hint of the friendliness he had shown her when he had taken her to tea at the Royal Oak Hotel on his haughty features.

'At no time did I abandon my grandmother.'

Emma stared at the floor and wished she could sink through it. Once again she had jumped to conclusions and judged Rocco unfairly. 'I had the impression from Cordelia that you had gone to Paris *after* her accident,' she mumbled. 'But she's in shock, and it's not surprising she's confused. I'm sorry,' she finished in a low tone.

She bit her lip. She might have misjudged him over Cordelia, but the fact remained that he *had* hot-footed it off to Paris to see his mistress, and had probably spent Sunday afternoon... She frantically tried to block out the image of him and the beautiful Mademoiselle Pascal naked on a bed, making love.

Acid burned in the pit of her stomach—indigestion, she reassured herself, not jealousy. Desperate to avoid looking at him, she busied herself with making a pot of tea.

'Well, anyway, you're back now.' She strove to sound brisk and efficient. 'When will the central heating be working again?'

'It won't,' Rocco informed her tersely. 'The problem is with the boiler, but the whole system is antiquated and needs replacing—which in a house this size could take weeks, if not months.'

Emma gave him a startled look. 'Cordelia can't stay here when there is no heating.'

'Of course not. I'm sure you agree that it is imperative I persuade her to come and stay at my home in Italy—by whatever means I can,' Rocco added obliquely as he picked up the tea tray and strode out of the kitchen.

Back in the sitting room, it became clear, when Emma poured the tea, that Cordelia was unable to hold a cup with her bruised fingers, and was struggling with her bandaged hand.

'Let me help you,' she said gently, feeling a wave of compassion for the elderly lady. Cordelia was so determined to hang on to her independence, but this latest accident had left her looking painfully frail.

Rocco stoked the fire and added another log, glad of the excuse to turn away from his grandmother for a few moments. It struck him forcibly that Nonna was in the twilight years of her life. For a moment his eyes stung, and he blinked hard, telling himself it was because of the smoke.

His mind drifted back to the past. It had been Nonna who had comforted him in the dark days after Gio's death, and who had insisted that the accident hadn't been his fault. He had overheard her telling his mother to stop blaming him, that Flora should have been responsible for her younger son rather than handing his care over to a teenage boy. His grandmother had been his friend and ally when he had needed her most. Now she needed him—and he would not fail her.

He stood and walked back across the room, his eyes drawn to Emma, who was patiently helping Cordelia to sip her tea. She might be a termagant with him, but the gentle compassion she showed his grandmother was a rare quality that moved him deeply.

Cordelia glanced at her injured hands and gave him a resigned look. 'This is a pretty kettle of fish, isn't it?'

'It is indeed, Nonna. But fortunately I have the ideal solution.' Rocco spoke firmly and without hesitation. 'Emma has agreed to come to Portofino to be your nurse while you are recovering from your various injuries. Naturally she will be bringing Holly with her,' he added, quickly reassuring the little girl, who had looked momentarily worried.

He saw Emma stiffen, but before she could say a word Cordelia gave her a beaming smile tinged with tangible relief. 'Oh, my dear—I can't tell you how delighted I am. Rocco has been trying to persuade me to go and stay with him, but he leads a busy life, and I was afraid I would be lonely. But if you and Holly are going to be with me we'll have a *lovely* holiday—before I come back to live at Nunstead,' she said, her tone as firm as Rocco's had been.

'We'll discuss that once you are fully recovered.' Rocco deemed it wise not to push his luck with his stubborn grandmother. Conscious that if the look in Emma's stormy eyes could kill, he would be dead by now, he focused on her daughter. 'Would you like to come to Italy and stay in my house by the sea?'

Holly nodded, her eyes as wide as saucers. 'Can we go in the sea?'

'The sun will soon be warm enough for us to go to

the beach, and you can play in the garden with Bobbo, my dog.'

Wonderful, Emma thought bitterly. If the promise of trips to the beach wasn't enough, Rocco had a dog. Holly would be in seventh heaven. She stared at her daughter's excited face and her heart sank. How could she disappoint an elderly lady and a small child by refusing to go to Italy? She glared at Rocco—who knew quite well that she could not.

'Can I have a private word with you, to discuss arrangements?' she murmured in a saccharine tone, so that Cordelia would not realise she wanted to murder her grandson.

'Of course.' Rocco gave her a bland smile. 'Why don't we step into the hall?'

'You are *unbelievable*,' she breathed, the moment she shut the sitting room door behind them.

'I'm not certain you mean that as a compliment, but thank you.'

Her fingers itched to wipe the amusement from his face. 'You know damn well it wasn't a compliment—just as you know my feelings about this trip to Portofino. I made my reasons clear as to why I can't go.'

'Actually, you failed to give any good reason for wanting to upset my grandmother and spoil Holly's excitement.'

'You had *no* right to use my daughter to try and get your own way. Emotional blackmail is unforgivable.'

He shrugged. 'In business, I'll use any means at my disposal to win a deal, and the same goes for my private life. I want you to look after Cordelia, and if I have to use a little coercion to get what I want, so be it.'

Beneath his charming façade there was a ruthless side to Rocco. He would make a dangerous adversary, Emma realised. But at the same time his loyalty and love for his grandmother were undeniable.

'If you are worried about your job here in Northumberland, it's fine. I've squared it for you,' he told her.

'What do you mean, you've *squared* it?'

'I spoke to the head of the trust you work for and arranged for you to have three months' unpaid leave. Mr Donaldson was most obliging—especially after I made a donation to the local cottage hospital.'

Far from being grateful that he had resolved a significant reason for her decision not to go to Portofino, Emma was furious at his interference. 'You treat people like puppets, don't you?' she snapped. 'You think your money gives you the right to arrange my life to suit you. If you want the truth, I don't *want* Holly to stay at your villa. A playboy's love nest is *not* a suitable environment for a child.'

While Rocco was absorbing this startling statement, she demanded, 'Will Juliette Pascal be there? Or another of your *lady friends*, as Cordelia euphemistically describes them? Maybe you plan to entertain more than one? From what I've heard, you frequently juggle multiple mistresses.'

'What an eye-watering vision you present,' Rocco drawled. He studied her flushed face speculatively. 'Juliette won't be visiting the Villa Lucia because I ended our affair yesterday. It wasn't really even an affair. We both lead busy lives and met up occasionally whenever we happened to be in the same city. It was an arrangement that suited both of us.'

After Rosalinda he had made sure any woman he dated understood unequivocally that there was no chance he would ever want more than a casual affair. He noted Emma's scathing expression and his jaw hardened.

'Despite what you may have read in the tabloid newspapers, I only ever have mistresses in multiples of one.

After kissing you on Saturday night, it was only right that I should end my relationship with Juliette. But I certainly wouldn't have done so with a phone call.'

Emma was struck dumb by his revelation. She felt a grudging respect that he had had the decency to end his affair in person. But had he slept with the beautiful model yesterday—enjoyed a final sex session for old times' sake? she wondered, feeling acid burn in the pit of her stomach.

'Why did you end your affair because of one kiss?' She strove to sound uninterested, not knowing that Rocco could see the uncertainty in her eyes. 'You said yourself there was no need to get worked up about it.' Unconsciously she worried the tender flesh of her lower lip with her teeth. 'It meant nothing to either of us.'

'Let's see, shall we?'

The sudden deepening of his voice should have triggered alarm bells, but he moved so quickly that she had no time to react. One arm snaked around her waist and pulled her hard up against him, while his other hand cupped her jaw as he covered her mouth with his.

This time his kiss was no gentle seduction. This time it was urgent and demanding, born of a sense of frustration—not only at Emma's stubbornness, but from the fact that ever since he had kissed her two nights ago all he had been able to think about was how soon he could repeat the experience. The feel of her soft curves pressed up against him heated his blood. Desire thundered through his veins, and he slid his hand from her jaw to tangle in her hair, tugging her head back so that he could plunder her soft, moist mouth.

Desperately, Emma fought the temptation to sink into him and lose herself in the mastery of his kiss. The logical part of her brain reminded her that she did not want this. She functioned perfectly well without passion and desire in her life. Those emotions had brought her nothing but heartache in the past and she would be a fool to be seduced by their sorcery. So *why*, instead of pushing Rocco away, did she slowly uncurl her clenched fists and lay her hands flat against his chest?

The determined probing of his tongue between her lips demolished her pitiful resistance and she gave a low moan as she opened her mouth for him, a tremor running through her when he explored her with devastating eroticism. Driven by a need she barely understood, she responded to him mindlessly.

Sensing her capitulation, he changed the tenure of the kiss so that it became a flagrant seduction of her senses. She shivered when she felt him slide his hand beneath the edge of her jumper to stroke her bare flesh lightly above the waistband of her jeans. Her skin felt acutely sensitised, so that the brush of his fingertips caused needle-darts of pleasure to shoot through her. Silently she willed him to skim his hand higher, to slip it beneath her bra and touch her naked breasts. Her nipples felt hot and swollen, and she was conscious of the moist secretion between her legs, the ache that could only be relieved by pressing her pelvis against his thighs.

She was utterly unprepared when he suddenly broke the kiss and lifted his head to stare down into her wide, stunned eyes. Realisation slowly dawned that she was clinging to him, and she snatched her hands from his body, scarlet colour flooding her face.

Attack was her only form of defence. *'How dare you?'*

He gave her a mocking look. 'Your outrage would have a little more impact if you had not responded to me so ardently.'

Rocco watched Emma pull the edge of her jumper firmly into place, feeling a curious tug on his heart when he saw that her hands were shaking. Her usually neat golden bob was mussed and had fallen forward across her cheek. He wanted to stroke her hair back from her face, but knew she would react like a wildcat if he attempted to touch her.

Fool, Emma berated herself furiously, closing her eyes as shame swept over her. It was bad enough that she had allowed him to kiss her, but to compound her stupidity she had kissed him back with embarrassing eagerness—until *he* had pulled back. She hadn't just responded to him ardently—she had practically eaten him alive!

Through the sitting room door she could hear Holly singing 'Twinkle Twinkle Little Star', her sweet voice joined by Cordelia's slightly wavering one. How could she walk back in and announce that she was *not* prepared to go to Italy as Cordelia's private nurse? The thought of the disappointment her words would cause made her wince. But how could she stay at Rocco's home after she had all but begged him to make love to her on the hall carpet? she wondered despairingly.

Taking a deep breath, she forced herself to meet his gaze. 'For Cordelia's sake I will come to Portofino.' Somehow she had to regain her dignity. 'I'll be happy to act as her nurse and companion, but I will *not* put up with you manhandling me.'

'If I had manhandled you, I promise you would not be standing there fully dressed, *cara*,' Rocco said dulcetly. Ignoring the daggers in her eyes, he reached into the pocket of his jeans and withdrew a slip of paper.

Frowning, Emma took the cheque from him, stared at it for a moment, and then back at him. 'I don't understand what this is for.'

'It's your salary for the next three months.'

'Don't be ridiculous. I earn this amount in a year.'

He shrugged. 'I want the best care for my grandmother. I know you will do everything possible to ensure she is comfortable and happy, and in return I am prepared to pay you well.'

'Not this well.' She shook her head briskly and tore the cheque in half. 'You don't have to offer me a bribe. I'm very fond of Cordelia and I want to look after her. All I require is the usual monthly salary I earn as a district nurse.'

Rocco stared at her in frustration. And he had thought his grandmother was strong-willed! Nonna was a pushover compared to Emma. 'But you could use the money as a deposit to buy Primrose Cottage.'

'*No.*' It was not even a consideration. 'Anyway, the cottage has already been sold. One day I'll have saved enough for a deposit on a house, but I'll pay my own way in life,' Emma said firmly. 'I don't want to feel indebted to anyone.' She hesitated. 'Neither do I want an affair with you. So if you were thinking you could pay me to…'

'*Madre de Dio!*' Rocco said harshly, his anger searing him like a white-hot branding iron. 'That is one insult too far, Emma. I have never *paid* for a woman in my life.' He stared at her haughtily, his skin stretched taut over his razor-sharp cheekbones, giving him a coldly autocratic appearance. 'I don't deny that I desire you, but when you come to my bed it will be of your own accord.'

His arrogance infuriated her, but she was even angrier with herself for the damning flare of excitement his words evoked.

'That's never going to happen.'

'Because you are still in love with your husband?' he speculated. Once again he struggled to contain his frustration—with him, with her, and most of all with the primitive need to possess her that made his gut ache. The world was full of attractive blondes who would be happy to share his bed. Why was he bothering with this feisty, stubborn woman who constantly challenged him?

Emma bit her lip, feeling an inexplicable urge to confide the truth about her marriage to Rocco. She could not, she reminded herself. For Holly's sake, Jack's duplicity must remain a secret. But her love for Jack had died with the discovery of how he had betrayed her. During the past three years she had come to terms with the hurt he had caused her, but her wariness and mistrust remained. Never again would she put herself in a position where her heart could be broken. She did not want any man in her life—certainly not a sexy Italian who regarded women as playthings.

'Jack is the reason why I refuse to get involved with you—or with any other man,' she said quietly.

'Do you think he would have wanted you to condemn yourself to a life alone?' Rocco demanded harshly.

'Maybe not, but I have Holly to consider. What do you suggest I do? Indulge in casual affairs, introduce her to a series of "uncles" who she may become close to, only to see her upset when they move on?'

'Of course not.' He raked a hand through his hair, appalled by the image she presented.

During his childhood his parents had both been openly unfaithful, and on the rare occasions when his mother had promised to visit him at his boarding school he had never been sure whether she would turn up with his father or one of her sleazeball boyfriends.

But, while he had taken scant interest in his parents' various lovers, it was likely that Holly, who had never known her own father, would welcome a father figure. Any man who became involved with Emma would need to recognise that he had a level of responsibility towards her child. A casual affair was out of the question—but that was all *he* could ever offer, Rocco thought grimly, all he would ever want.

His parents' volatile relationship had shown him that marriage was a gamble, with low odds of success. He was still haunted by Rosalinda's suicide attempt after he had ended their affair, and since then had made it clear at the outset with the women he dated that he was not looking for commitment or a long-term relationship. That meant that Emma was off-limits. She would not consider indulging in a brief sexual fling, and he could not help but respect her for her decision. Unlike his mother, Emma put the welfare of her child before her own desires.

The sitting room door suddenly opened and Holly appeared, happily oblivious to the tense atmosphere in the hall. 'Nonna and me want to know when we are going to stay at your house,' she asked Rocco.

'Tomorrow.' He ignored Emma's sharply indrawn breath and smiled at the little girl.

Big grey eyes, so like her mother's, studied him anxiously. 'Is Thomas coming too?'

'No. Cats don't like travelling on aeroplanes, so he is going to stay at Yaxley Farm.'

When Holly trotted off to relay this information to Cordelia, Emma glared at Rocco. Panic gripped her. She was backtracking fast, bitterly regretting the moment of insanity that had seen her agree to go to Italy with him. 'I can't possibly be ready to leave tomorrow. There are dozens of things to do, arrangements to be made...'

'All you have to do is pack yours and Holly's things. Make a list of anything else that needs to be done and my PA will take care of everything. Stop looking for difficulties that don't exist,' Rocco told her tersely. 'Because of the broken heating system I'm taking Cordelia to spend the night at the Royal Oak Hotel. But it's not ideal. I want to take her to Portofino as soon as possible.'

'But…' Emma found she was speaking to thin air as he strode past her into the sitting room.

Irritating man, she fumed. All her instincts were screaming at her to tell him she had changed her mind. But it was too late now; she could not upset Cordelia and Holly. It was only for three months, she reminded herself. Three months of living in Rocco's villa and seeing him every day, taunted a little voice inside her head. She could only pray she survived with her emotions unscathed.

CHAPTER SIX

'Look, Mummy. The sea!' Holly burst through the connecting door between her bedroom and Emma's at the Villa Lucia, and pointed excitedly towards the window. 'It's blue,' she observed, pressing her nose to the glass.

'It certainly is—almost as blue as the sky. Isn't it beautiful?' As Emma joined her daughter at the window she could not help but compare the sparkling cobalt waters in the Bay of Tigullio with the steel-grey surf that had pounded the shore on the coast of Northumberland the last time she had taken Holly for a trip to the beach.

Rocco's villa was built on a hillside, affording a panoramic view of picturesque Portofino, the wide sweep of the bay and the surrounding mountains, which were densely covered with pine trees and other foliage so that the landscape was a lush, verdant green. Directly in front of the house was a series of terraced gardens, and on the lower level was a huge pool which sparkled invitingly in the bright sunshine. Lower still could be seen Portofino's port, where dozens of boats were moored in neat rows. Pretty, pastel-coloured buildings ringed the harbour, the shopfronts shaded by striped awnings which fluttered in the breeze.

'Shall we go swimming now?'

Emma smiled at Holly's hopeful expression. 'Not for

a few days—at least not in the sea,' she said gently. 'Remember, Rocco said the sea will be too cold to swim in yet? But when your cough is better you can go in the pool, because the water is heated.'

'There's Bobbo!' Holly was distracted from the subject of swimming when she spied a chocolate-coloured Labrador hurtling across the lawn. 'Rocco said I can give Bobbo his breakfast,' she said joyfully.

'After you've eaten all *your* breakfast,' Emma told her firmly.

She sighed. Holly had fallen in love with Rocco's dog within five minutes of their arrival at the Villa Lucia the previous evening. Added to that, the little girl seemed to hero-worship Rocco, and Emma was already worried about how upset her daughter was going to be when it was time for them to return to England. But there was no point in thinking about that now, she told herself as she stared out of the window, her gaze focused not on the dog but on the tall, athletic man who was throwing a ball for the animal.

She guessed from Rocco's attire of shorts, vest top and trainers that he had been running. His sports clothes revealed his superb physique: broad shoulders, rippling biceps and muscular thighs. His satiny skin was tanned a deep olive colour, and his hair gleamed jet-black, like a raven's wing in the sunlight.

He was a work of art, she acknowledged ruefully. But, unlike any marble statue sculpted by Michelangelo, Rocco was a flesh-and-blood man. Not for the first time Emma found herself remembering how it had felt when he had pulled her into his arms and ravaged her mouth with his own. He had demanded a response she had been helpless to deny, and the memory of his kiss caused her nipples to harden, so that they rubbed uncomfortably against her lacy bra.

To her horror he suddenly glanced up at the house and lifted his hand in greeting. Holly waved excitedly back at him, but Emma hurriedly stepped away from the window, feeling horribly embarrassed that she had been caught ogling him. Rocco could not possibly have known that she had been imagining him stripping out of his running gear and stepping naked beneath a shower, sliding a bar of soap over the hard muscles of his abdomen and then lower...

'Come on, we must go and see if Cordelia needs any help, and then we'll all go down for breakfast,' she told Holly briskly. With any luck Rocco would take some time to shower and dress, and there was a good chance she would be able to avoid meeting him before he left for work.

So far, her plan to have as little contact with him as possible had been surprisingly successful. She even had a niggling suspicion that he was equally keen to keep their relationship to a strictly employer/employee basis. During the flight to Genoa aboard his private jet he had been exquisitely polite towards her, but distinctly aloof. There had been no hint of his sexy charm, no flirtatious glances, and his warm smile had been reserved for his grandmother and Holly.

It was exactly what she wanted, Emma assured herself. She had come to the Villa Lucia in a purely professional role, to act as Cordelia's nurse, and she was glad Rocco recognised that fact. The flat feeling inside her was probably a reaction to the previous twenty-four hours, when she had been busy packing everything she'd thought Holly would need for their stay in Italy, plus a small suitcase containing her own few belongings.

Holding Holly by the hand, she led the way along the corridor to Cordelia's room where she discovered that the elderly lady needed help fastening the buttons on her dress.

'Your burn looks so much better this morning that I

should be able to remove the dressing tomorrow,' Emma told her. 'Without the bandages you'll have more mobility in your fingers, but I'm afraid the fingers on your other hand are still very swollen, and it's going to take a while for the bruising to fade.'

'That's what comes of being a foolish old woman,' Cordelia said despondently. 'I've made such a nuisance of myself to everyone—especially Rocco.'

'No one could ever accuse you of being foolish,' Emma reassured her gently. 'And Rocco is delighted you've come to stay with him.'

His love for his grandmother had been evident in the tender way he had taken care of her during the flight to Italy the previous day. This softer side to his commanding personality was unexpected, and Emma was still embarrassed that she had accused him of being uncaring the first time she had met him.

They took the lift down to the ground floor. The villa was built on four levels, and it was doubtful Cordelia would have managed so many stairs. Rocco had confided to Emma that he had had the lift installed a couple of years ago, when he had realised that his grandmother could not continue to live alone at Nunstead Hall. Far from shirking his responsibility, he had clearly planned to take care of Cordelia in the last years of her life.

They were greeted by the cook, Beatrice, who chatted volubly in a mixture of Italian and broken English as she ushered them into the breakfast room, which overlooked the gardens and the sapphire sea sparkling in the distance.

'I bake rolls fresh this morning, and there is fruit and yogurt. If you need anything else for the *bambina* you ask Beatrice, *si*?' she said earnestly.

'*Grazie*. I'm sure we have everything we need,' Emma replied, taken aback by the wonderful selection of fresh fruit set out on the table. She was even more surprised when Holly and Cordelia both ate hearty breakfasts. It was probably the result of the antibiotics, but Holly was not coughing nearly as much, and for the first time in weeks there was a faint tinge of pink on her cheeks.

'*Buongiorno*, ladies.' Rocco strolled into the room and bent his head to kiss his grandmother's cheek. 'Nonna, Holly…Emma.' Was it her imagination, or had his voice cooled fractionally as he had spoken her name? 'I am glad you are here in my home.'

To her self-disgust the sight of him made her heart-rate quicken, and she busied herself with wiping yogurt from Holly's face while she struggled to regain her composure. It did not help that Rocco looked devastatingly gorgeous in beige chinos and a black polo shirt, his damp hair an indication that he had recently showered. She had assumed that as the CEO of a world-famous company he would wear a suit to work, and Cordelia must have shared her thoughts.

The elderly lady studied her grandson. 'Don't tell me you are one of those trendy executives who chooses not to wear a tie to the office, Rocco?'

'Certainly not,' he murmured, his lazy smile doing strange things to Emma's insides. 'But I'm not going to work today. I want to make sure my guests settle in to the Villa Lucia.' His golden eyes trapped Emma's gaze. 'Did you sleep well?'

Her cool smile disguised her intense awareness of him. 'Very, thank you.' He could not know that she had spent another restless night during which she had been unable to dismiss him from her mind.

'If you've finished eating, I'd like a word with you.'

Without waiting for her to reply he turned and strode out of the door, leaving her with little option but to follow him out to the hall and across to his study.

'Why are you wearing your nurse's uniform?' he demanded, the moment she entered the room.

Emma's brows lifted fractionally at the abruptness of his tone. 'Because I am your grandmother's nurse.'

'Your role here is to act as Cordelia's companion. I hardly think that necessitates wearing a uniform. I would prefer you to wear normal clothes.'

She compressed her lips. 'But *I* would prefer to wear the uniform which denotes that I am your employee.' It was vital to her peace of mind that she distance herself from him. Her uniform signified that she was staying at his home in a professional capacity, and in some strange way she felt safe and in control when she was dressed in her work clothes. 'I think it is important to establish boundaries. I have accepted a contract to work for you, and I believe I should dress appropriately.'

Rocco trailed his eyes over Emma's plain blue dress, adorned only with an elasticated belt which showed off her slim waist and emphasised the delightful curves of her bust and hips, before lowering his gaze to her shapely legs, covered in sheer black hose and her sensible black shoes. No one could accuse her of dressing like a *femme fatale*, yet he was consumed with an extremely inappropriate urge to wrench open the front of her dress and feast his eyes on her bountiful breasts.

He shifted in his seat in an effort to ease the lustful throb in his groin. 'It doesn't seem to have occurred to you that Cordelia might not want people to know she has a nurse. My grandmother is fiercely proud. She has accepted the idea of having a companion, but she would hate people to think she is unable to care for herself.'

Emma bit her lip as Rocco's words struck a chord. It was true she had been so busy thinking about herself that she had not considered her patient's feelings. 'I appreciate what you're saying,' she mumbled. 'But Cordelia doesn't actually know anyone in Portofino, so who are all these people whose opinion she might worry about?'

'That's the other reason I asked to speak to you. I'm thinking of hosting a cocktail party and inviting friends and neighbours, perhaps a few colleagues from Eleganza, to welcome Nonna to Italy. Do you think it would be too much for her?' He exhaled heavily. 'She looks so frail, and I don't want to overtire her.'

'I think Cordelia would love a party in her honour,' Emma assured him. 'She often talks about the parties she and her husband used to give at Nunstead Hall years ago. She would enjoy the chance to dress up, and I can help her to get ready.'

'You will, of course, accompany her to the party.'

The prospect of socialising with Rocco's glamorous friends made Emma's heart sink. It had struck her yesterday, when she had stepped onto his luxurious private jet, that their lives were light years apart, and she did not belong in his rarefied world of the super-rich. 'Surely that won't be necessary? I'll be on hand, of course, but—as you said yourself—Cordelia doesn't need a nurse in constant attendance.'

'*Dio*, Emma, why is everything a battle with you?' Rocco's patience snapped. 'You are a guest in my home and naturally you are included in my invitation to the party. Why are you so determined to reject any overtures of friendship from me?' His eyes narrowed on her startled face. 'You seem to be afraid to trust. But why? Who caused you to be so wary?'

'No one.' Her tone was defensive, and she flushed when he gave her a sardonic look. Emma took a deep breath. 'I'm sure we can establish a cordial friendship for the duration of my stay at the Villa Lucia.'

What was she thinking behind her cool grey gaze? Rocco wondered frustratedly. He was tempted to spread her across his desk, shove her starched nurse's dress up to her waist and prove emphatically that she no more wanted a *cordial friendship* than he did.

'Were you happy with Jack?' he asked abruptly, his sharp gaze noting how she tensed at the mention of her husband.

'Yes, of course.'

It was a partial truth, Emma acknowledged silently. Blissfully unaware that Jack had been unfaithful from the first weeks of their marriage, she had believed they were happy. There had been a few issues that had caused her concern—mainly his irresponsibility with money. She had quickly learned to put her wages away to pay the rent and bills, because Jack could blow his month's salary in a single shopping trip. He could not help his impulsive nature, she had told herself. Blinded by her love for him, she had made excuses for his selfishness—even in the bedroom, when he had often taken his own pleasure without any consideration for hers. He was tired after working a long shift, she had told herself, not knowing that he had been with his mistress, rather than on duty at the fire station.

Looking back, she despised herself for having been such a naive fool. It was not only other people that she now found hard to trust, but her faith in her own judgement had been shattered. She stared at Rocco's impossibly handsome face and felt her stomach dip. He had awoken her libido and made her long for the warmth and closeness of making love. But that closeness had been an illusion with Jack, and it could not exist with Rocco, who was the ultimate playboy.

'Getting back to the party,' she said quickly, desperate to steer the conversation away from her marriage. 'I don't have anything suitable to wear. I don't get invited to many cocktail parties in Little Copton,' she added dryly.

Rocco shrugged. 'That's not a problem. Portofino is renowned for its designer boutiques. We'll go shopping this afternoon, and I'll look after Holly while you try on dresses. Don't argue, Emma,' he warned, seeing the glint of battle in her eyes. 'Holly will enjoy a trip to the harbour. I've already asked Cordelia if she would like to come, but she says she's weary today and so she'll stay here with Beatrice.'

'You seem to have arranged everything—as usual.' Struggling to control her temper, Emma turned on her heels to march out of his study, but in her haste she banged her hip against the desk and knocked a framed photograph to the floor. 'Sorry,' she muttered as she stooped to retrieve it, thankful to see that the glass had not broken.

She studied the picture of two dark-haired boys. The older was clearly Rocco—even as a teenager he had been stunningly good-looking, she noted. The younger boy bore a strong resemblance to Rocco, and Emma suddenly remembered that he had mentioned he had a sibling.

'Will your brother be at the party?'

'No.'

Startled by his curt response, she looked at him and glimpsed a sudden bleakness in his eyes.

'Giovanni died a week after that picture was taken.'

Shocked, she stared back at the photo. 'I'm sorry. He was just a child.'

'Seven years old,' Rocco revealed emotionlessly.

Emma wanted to ask more, but Rocco's closed expression warned her he did not want to discuss his brother's death. He jerked to his feet and strode across the room to open the door. 'I need to work for a couple of hours, so I'll have to ask you to go back to my grandmother.'

'Yes, of course.' Summarily dismissed, she had no option but to stifle her curiosity and walk out of the study.

Rocco closed the study door and leaned against it, his eyes focused on the photograph Emma had handed to him. Even after twenty years he still felt an ache in his heart when he thought of Gio, and the guilt that he was partly responsible for his brother's death would always be with him. But fate worked in mysterious ways, he brooded. He had lost Gio, but now he had a brother again.

Marco was the image of Gio. And Marco needed him—just as Gio had. Although at the moment his little half-brother—his father's illegitimate son—was full of anger and confusion, and defiantly resistant to Rocco's attempts to build a relationship with him. But slowly, with patience, he would do his best to win the little boy round. Marco needed a father figure, and Rocco had vowed to give his brother the guidance and love that he would have given Gio.

For the time being, though, he had decided to keep Marco's identity hidden. There would be huge interest once it became known that Enrico D'Angelo had had a secret son, and Rocco was determined to protect his brother from the media sharks who would circle once the story broke.

'This is pointless,' Emma muttered that afternoon, as she trailed after Rocco along Portofino's main street and halted next to him outside another boutique. She glanced at the window display and her eyebrows shot up when she saw the price tag attached to the exquisite gown draped on the mannequin. 'I can't afford designer clothes.'

The Via Roma was lined with exclusive boutiques and jewellers, interspersed with local shops selling beautiful handmade goods, and art galleries stacked with paintings depicting the stunning scenery of the bay of Tigullio.

Portofino was known as the Italian Riviera—a mecca for the rich and beautiful—and Emma, wearing old jeans and a sweatshirt, which were the only clothes she possessed other than her nurse's uniform, felt decidedly out of place.

'I'm not going to find a dress here,' she told Rocco, who looked every inch a multi-millionaire business tycoon in his expertly tailored clothes and designer shades. 'You and I come from different worlds, and I am very much a discount store girl. I'm going to take Holly to see the boats in the harbour. Come on, munchkin,' she said, resisting the urge to prise her daughter's fingers out of Rocco's grasp. She had felt a sharp pang when Holly had happily held Rocco's hand and skipped along beside him. She was worried her little girl would get too attached, and it would break her heart when the time came to leave.

'I think Mummy should try on that pink dress,' Rocco said to Holly. 'Princesses wear pink dresses, don't they?'

She nodded, big grey eyes sparkling with excitement. 'You can be a princess, Mummy—like Cinderella.'

'Doesn't it bother your conscience to know you are manipulating a small child?' Emma hissed, giving him a glare that would have floored a lesser man.

'I don't have a conscience, *cara*.' Rocco grinned unrepentantly as he pushed open the shop door and ushered her inside. He spoke in Italian to the elegant assistant, while Emma hovered, feeling horribly conscious that her faded jeans were hardly couture. She had no idea what he said, but within minutes the assistant had brought out a selection of dresses for her to try on.

'I'll take Holly to buy an ice cream,' he murmured. 'Here's my credit card. Choose a couple of dresses and charge them to my account.'

'You must be joking. You're not going to pay for my clothes.'

'Think of it as a requirement for your job,' he advised smoothly. 'I want you at Cordelia's party, so don't leave here without something to wear.'

'*Signorina* does not like it?' the assistant queried ten minutes later, as Emma handed back the dress that she had seen displayed in the window.

'It's absolutely beautiful,' she assured the woman. 'But I can't afford it.' Made of pale pink chiffon, with narrow diamanté shoulder straps, the dress was a masterpiece of understated elegance. Emma had fallen in love with it the moment she had slipped it over her head, but it cost a fortune, and whatever Rocco said she was not going to allow him to buy it for her. Instead, she hurried out of the designer boutique and walked back to a shop which stocked clothes closer to her price range. The navy blue dress in the window was smart and practical. She would probably get years of wear out of it, she consoled herself as she handed the assistant her own credit card.

To Emma's relief, Rocco went to work for the rest of the week, driving to Eleganza's head office in the city of Genoa, some fifteen miles from Portofino. He left the Villa Lucia early each morning, and returned to dine with his grandmother in the evening. He insisted that Emma ate with them, dismissing her argument that Cordelia might want to spend time alone with her grandson.

'Anyone would think you are reluctant to be in my company,' he had taunted softly on that first evening, when he'd demanded her presence in the dining room. 'What are you afraid of, Emma? How can we become friends if you constantly avoid me?'

'I'm not afraid of you,' she denied sharply, the sultry gleam in his golden eyes making her feel hot and flustered.

She looked at him uncertainly. 'Is that what you want—for us to be friends?'

His sensual smile stole her breath. 'I would be lying if I said that was *all* I wanted, *cara*. But it's a start.'

In truth, Rocco did not know what he wanted. The simple answer was Emma—in his bed. His desire for her was like a ravenous beast, eating away at him, distracting his mind during the day and keeping him awake at night as he fantasised about the many and varied ways he would enjoy possessing her delectable body.

If she had been any other woman he would have wasted no time seducing her. But Emma was unlike any woman he had ever met. For one thing she was a widow who still mourned the husband she had loved—which made the vulnerable expression in her eyes whenever Jack Marchant's name was mentioned puzzling, Rocco brooded.

Now, at the end of the week, he felt as wound up as a coiled spring. Sexual frustration was not conducive to a good mood, he'd discovered. There were several women he could call—casual mistresses who would be happy to join him for dinner at an exclusive restaurant followed by a night of mutually enjoyable sex, with no strings attached. So why wasn't he tempted to pick up the phone? Why did he feel jaded by a diet of sophisticated lovers and meaningless physical encounters?

The answer could be found in a pair of grey eyes that regarded him coolly across the dinner table every evening. Sometimes the expression in those eyes was not as dismissive as he suspected their owner wished. Emma was fighting the sexual chemistry between them. But it was there, simmering beneath the surface of their polite conversation, and blazing in the stolen glances they shared. He heard her swiftly indrawn breath when he leaned close to refill her wine glass, and he knew they both felt a tingle of electricity if their hands accidentally brushed.

Their attraction to one another was undeniable, but for the first time in his life Rocco could not simply take what he wanted. Beneath Emma's crisp, no-nonsense exterior he had glimpsed a woman of deep emotions, gentle, compassionate, and possessing an air of vulnerability that tugged on his insides. And there was her daughter to consider. Holly was an enchanting child, who looked at him with such innocent trust in her eyes that he already felt fiercely protective of her. He would do anything to avoid hurting her, or her mother.

Rocco's staff had become used to him leaving the office early on Friday afternoons. There was much speculation as to where he went, the general consensus being that he must go to meet a mistress, but the gossipers were careful to keep their thoughts to themselves whenever Eleganza's CEO was in earshot.

As he drove through the heavy traffic to the other side of Genoa, the last thing on Rocco's mind was office tittle-tattle about his private life. When he pulled up outside Marco's school there were only a few kids hanging around, including a small boy with jet-black hair and unusual amber-coloured eyes, who trudged over to the car with obvious reluctance and a dark scowl on his face.

'I'm sorry I'm late. There was a snarl-up on the Via Serra.' Rocco stifled a sigh when his brother climbed into the front passenger seat and flicked him a glance of supreme indifference. The way the boy folded his arms across his chest was instinctively defensive, and revealed a vulnerability that made Rocco want to reach out to him.

'I told you—you don't have to come. I walk home every

other day.' Marco darted him a quick glance. 'I thought you weren't coming—and I wouldn't have cared.'

Beneath the belligerence Rocco caught a note of uncertainty in the little boy's voice and his heart clenched. 'I'll always come on Fridays. I would never let you down,' he promised quietly.

Golden eyes glared at him from beneath the untidy mop of hair—eyes that were shadowed with hurt that should not be borne by a seven-year-old. It was hardly surprising, Rocco thought heavily. Up until four months ago Marco had not known that he was the son of Enrico D'Angelo, or that he had an older half-brother. What had induced Enrico to ask to meet his illegitimate son as he lay dying Rocco did not understand. Possibly his father had felt remorseful that he had abandoned his one-time mistress when she had fallen pregnant with his child. But Marco had only seen his father once before Enrico had died. The boy was clearly traumatised, resentful and touchingly protective of his mother who had struggled to bring him up without any financial support from her wealthy ex-lover.

'Why do you come?' Marco burst out. 'Me and Mamma didn't need Enrico, and we don't need you.'

'You are my brother, and I want to visit you,' Rocco said gently. 'It was wrong of our father to turn his back on you, and it is my duty to help your mother take care of you while you are growing up. But, more than that, I want us to be friends, Marco.'

He hesitated, thinking of his recent conversation with Inga Salveson, who had been his father's mistress. 'Your mother has told me she is thinking about moving back to Sweden, and of course you would go with her. But that will only happen if you decide that you do not want anything to do with me and your grandfather here in Italy. It's your choice whether or not you want to be a D'Angelo.'

For the first time there was a glimmer of curiosity in the wary golden eyes. 'Does my grandfather know about me?'

'No—not yet. Silvio is an old man, who has been ill recently. I don't want to tell him he has another grandson until you are sure you would like to meet him. It would be upsetting for him if you decided not to.'

Marco's lower lip wobbled betrayingly. 'I don't know what to do.' Tears clung perilously to his lower lashes. All his defiance suddenly disappeared, leaving behind a small, confused little boy. 'My *papà* is dead and I didn't even know him,' he choked. 'Don't tell my *nonno* about me yet…but maybe I will want to meet him one day. I will want to meet him.' A tear overspilled and slid down his cheek.

Rocco swallowed the constriction that had formed in his throat, his anger at Enrico's irresponsibility turning to compassion for this little boy who had met his father briefly and then lost him for ever. It was not surprising that Marco was so mistrustful.

Throwing aside his usual caution when dealing with his brother, he put his arm around Marco's shoulders. 'Whatever you want, Marco,' he said softly. 'I promise I won't tell anyone you are Enrico's son until you are happy for me to do so. Now…' he smiled, trying to break the tension '…how about we go and get some ice-cream?'

'Okay.' Marco scrubbed his wet face with a grubby hand. And for the first time he returned his brother's smile.

Preparations were in full swing when Rocco arrived back at the Villa Lucia that evening. He frequently hosted social events, and his staff, under Beatrice's command, could be trusted to ensure that the cocktail party in his grandmother's honour ran smoothly. He headed straight for his room to shower and change, before going back downstairs.

Beatrice had excelled herself, he noted. The Villa Lucia looked beautiful and welcoming. Huge vases of roses and lilies decorated the entrance hall and reception rooms, filling the air with their heady fragrance, while dozens of flickering candles emitted a golden glow. In fifteen minutes the guests would begin to arrive. The champagne was on ice, and the kitchen staff would serve a selection of canapés.

It had been a good day—especially as he felt he had made a break-through with Marco. Feeling a pleasant sense of well-being, Rocco was about to join his grandmother in the sitting room when a terse voice stopped him in his tracks.

'Where are my clothes?'

He turned to see Emma marching down the wide staircase, and even across the distance of the hall he noted that her eyes were the colour of storm clouds.

'Don't even think about making one of your clever remarks,' she warned him as he subjected her to a leisurely inspection. 'This dress does not belong to me, and neither do any of the other designer clothes that have appeared in my wardrobe.'

Emma took a deep breath, trying to control the fury that had swiftly followed her shock when she had gone to change into the navy dress she had bought for the party and discovered that her own clothes had disappeared and been replaced with dozens of beautiful outfits—many of which she had tried on during her shopping trip with Rocco a few days ago. 'What are you playing at, Rocco?'

'I bought you the clothes because you can't spend the next three months wearing jeans and a sweatshirt,' he explained mildly. 'For one thing, you don't need winter clothes here. The temperature is likely to shoot up in the summer.' He trailed his eyes over her, from her silky strawberry-blonde bob down to her slim shoulders revealed by the narrow straps of the pink cocktail dress. 'Besides, it's a crime to hide your gorgeous figure beneath bulky, shapeless garments.'

The bodice of the dress was cleverly cut so that her breasts were lifted high, their creamy upper slopes displayed in all their bounteous glory. Rocco's mouth went dry as he pictured himself drawing the straps down until those firm mounds of flesh spilled into his hands. He dropped his gaze lower, noting how the delicate chiffon skirt skimmed the curve of her hips and stopped several inches above her knees. Strappy silver shoes with three-inch heels accentuated the slender length of her legs.

'Sei bella,' he said roughly, colour flaring along his cheekbones. Desire ripped through him, shocking in its intensity, and he was conscious of the erection straining uncomfortably beneath his trousers. 'I knew the dress would suit you, but you have surpassed all my expectations, cara.' So much so that he was gripped with a fierce urge to carry her upstairs to his room and peel the dress from her body before making hard, urgent love to her. But there was his grandmother, the party, his duty as host. However much he wished that he was alone with Emma, he had to control his hunger for her—not least because of the wariness in her eyes.

'The clothes are a measure of my appreciation for the way you cared for Cordelia in Northumberland, and my thanks that you agreed to accompany her to Italy.'

She shook her head. 'I can't accept them. It's enough that you pay me a salary.'

Emma could not disguise the note of panic in her voice. She did not want to feel indebted to Rocco. Ever since she had met him she had felt that her life was spinning out of control. As a single mother she had never had spare money to spend on herself, and she could only ever have dreamed of owning the exquisite creation she was wearing. But the dress did not belong to her—and she did not belong here in Rocco's luxurious home.

'Is it so hard for you to accept a gift?'

The gentle note in his voice undermined her defences and sudden tears stung her eyes. She felt an inexplicable urge to confide in him that Jack had ruined her pleasure in receiving gifts. He had frequently given her presents, and naively she had taken his generosity as a sign of his love for her. But after his death she had realised that the flowers and perfume he'd lavished on her had been a way of assuaging his conscience after he had slept with one of his many mistresses.

She closed her eyes, trying to block out the memory of the pain and hurt Jack had caused her. When she opened them again Rocco was still there, devastatingly handsome in superbly tailored black trousers and a white silk shirt, a lock of dark hair falling across his brow and his golden eyes watching her with the intentness of a tiger stalking its prey.

'What do you want from me?' she whispered despairingly.

He lifted his hand and smoothed her hair back from her cheek. His touch was as light as the brush of a butterfly's wing against her skin, yet she felt as though she had been branded by him.

It was no longer the truth to say that sexual satisfaction and the sating of desire was all he wanted. Perhaps it never had been with this woman, Rocco owned silently.

'A chance to try and win your trust,' he said steadily.

'*Why?*' A wealth of fear and confusion was in that one

word. Emma blinked back the tears that threatened to over-spill, unaware that their shimmer made Rocco's gut clench. 'You can have any woman you want.' She had fallen for a handsome playboy once before. She could *not* make the same mistake again.

'I want you.' His voice was thick with need as he slid his hand to her nape. A warning voice inside Emma's head told her she should move—*now*. But Rocco's golden eyes were mesmerising, and she stared into them helplessly as his head descended.

The kiss was as gentle as thistledown, with an unex-pected tenderness that tugged on her soul. Bewitching, beguiling, he moved his lips over hers with sensual delib-eration, his hungry passion simmering but held in check—just.

Emma trembled as he drew her against him, silently acknowledging that she was losing the battle with her-self. *This* was where she wanted to be—in his arms, his mouth warm on hers, eliciting a response she was pow-erless to withhold. Slowly she lifted her arms and linked them around his neck. The sound of his low groan as she parted her lips beneath his sent a shiver of sexual excite-ment down her spine.

The crunch of tyres on the gravel driveway at the front of the house, followed by car doors closing and the indis-tinct babble of voices, drove Rocco to break the kiss re-luctantly. His timing was appalling, he thought grimly as he stared into Emma's smoke-soft eyes and watched them widen as panic replaced the sensual languor of a few sec-onds ago.

'Will you at least believe that I would never knowingly hurt you?' he said intently as he released her. He watched her unconsciously catch her lower lip with her teeth, and exhaled heavily. 'I must go and greet my guests.'

His words impelled her to action and she spun away from him towards the stairs. 'I'll go and check on Holly.' The little girl had fallen asleep soon after being tucked into bed, but the excuse would give Emma vital minutes to regain her composure.

The mirror on the first floor landing revealed the extent of the damage Rocco had wrought. Her eyes were over-bright, her mouth softly swollen. She took a tube of pale pink gloss from her purse and with a shaking hand reapplied it to her lips.

Trust! She gave a ragged laugh. Rocco did not know what he asked of her. After Jack, she had believed she would never have faith in any man ever again. But Rocco had sworn that he did not want to hurt her. He had offered her friendship, although the hungry desire in his eyes promised more.

For three years she had hidden away in a remote Northumberland village and focused all her attention on her daughter. It had been a safe existence, although sometimes a lonely one, she admitted. Rocco had forced her to see that she did not want to hide away for ever. But did she have the nerve to step out of her safety zone and risk her emotional stability by becoming involved with him?

CHAPTER SEVEN

To Emma's relief, the guests at Cordelia's party were not all glamorous and sophisticated. Rocco had invited friends and neighbours of a wide age range, including a retired English couple who had moved to Italy some years previously.

'We know Nunstead Hall. We saw it when we toured Northumbria a few years ago,' Barbara Harris exclaimed. 'We're actually just along the coast at Rapallo. There's quite a few of us ex-pats living there. Andrew and I hold a bridge evening once a week, and we'd love you to join us, Cordelia.'

'Thank you.' Rocco's grandmother looked delighted. 'I do enjoy playing card games. I used to belong to a bridge club in the village, but now that I don't drive I can no longer get there.' She smiled ruefully. 'It will be nice to have some company. Nunstead is rather remote.'

Coming to Portofino had been the best thing for Cordelia, Emma mused. The elderly lady already seemed less frail, after a week of sitting in the garden in the warm spring sunshine, and eating the wonderful meals served by Beatrice. She knew Rocco hoped to persuade his grandmother to stay at the Villa Lucia permanently, and Cordelia seemed to be settling in so quickly that perhaps she would not need a private nurse for much longer.

Once she returned to England she would probably never see Rocco again. The thought hurt Emma more than it should. *Don't*, her mind warned her. Don't dwell on that sweetly evocative kiss they had shared moments before the party. Rocco had kissed her because he wanted to sleep with her, and she could not deny that he had awoken her sensuality from a deep slumber. But if she did have an affair with him—and it was a big if—she must never forget that it would be a brief sexual adventure that could mean nothing to either of them.

He was standing on the other side of the room, chatting to neighbours who lived in a villa farther down the hill and their attractive young daughter. Perhaps he possessed a sixth sense which alerted him to Emma's scrutiny, for he suddenly turned his head and trapped her gaze. Colour flooded her face—embarrassment that he had caught her staring at him mixed with a fierce sexual awareness that sent a tremor of longing through her. His magnetism was so powerful that the other people in the room faded to the periphery of her vision and the murmur of voices, the clink of glasses on the silver trays carried by the villa staff, became muted.

How could she even contemplate an affair with him when he had the ability to decimate her composure with one look across a crowded room? she thought despairingly. The risk was too great. Perhaps it would be different if she only had herself to consider. But there was Holly, who already regarded Rocco as a friend. Her little daughter would be upset when he abruptly disappeared out of their lives, as he surely would when their relationship had run its course.

'Our host *is* gorgeous, isn't he?' drawled a voice.

Desperately trying to school her features to hide her inner turmoil, she glanced at the woman who had come to stand beside her and offered a polite smile. Shayna Manzzini's husband, Tino, was an executive at Eleganza, and a close friend of Rocco's. Emma had taken an instant liking to friendly Tino, but had not warmed to his Canadian wife. Shayna had given up a modelling career when she had married, but still retained a stunning figure. The elegant brunette was undeniably beautiful, but her hard features were set in an expression of permanent dissatisfaction, and there was a brittle quality about her.

'Poor little fool,' Shayna said mockingly. 'Any woman who hopes Rocco will fall in love with them is destined for disappointment. The tiger will never be tamed.'

For a moment Emma was mortified, thinking that Shayna was referring to *her*, before she realised that the Canadian woman was looking across the room at the daughter of Rocco's neighbours. The girl was probably seventeen or eighteen, incredibly pretty, and clearly overwhelmed by Rocco's charisma. Her eyes were fixed on his face and she frequently tossed her glossy black curls over her shoulders. Her flirting skills were not yet refined.

'Chiara doesn't have a hope,' Shayna continued in her derisive drawl. 'Rocco isn't interested in *bambini*. But give her a couple of years and she might capture his interest for a week or two.' She glanced at Emma, her scarlet-glossed lips forming a tight smile. 'We were lovers briefly—a few years ago. Rocco's affairs are always brief,' she added sardonically. 'I saw the end coming and decided to settle for Tino. Definitely a case of second-best.' She shrugged her narrow shoulders. 'But a modelling career doesn't last for ever, and although Tino isn't of multi-millionaire status, he's still loaded.'

Shocked by the other woman's calculating nature, Emma could not think of anything to say. Images of Shayna and Rocco as lovers filled her mind and her stomach churned. How many other women here tonight were his ex-mistresses? she wondered as she scanned the room and focused on several exceptionally beautiful female guests.

She remembered how at Jack's funeral she had looked around the church and tried to guess which women he had slept with during their marriage. Her grief at his death had been mixed with anger and humiliation and agonising hurt, and she had vowed never to lay herself open to that level of pain ever again.

'It's a pity Rosalinda Barinelli didn't understand Rocco's "no commitment at any price rule."' Shayna's voice once again broke into Emma's thoughts.

'What do you mean?' She could not disguise her curiosity, even though she had a horrible feeling she was not going to like the Canadian woman's reply. 'Who is Rosalinda Barinelli?'

'She is, or rather *was*, a talented Italian actress with a promising career ahead of her. That was until she met Rocco. A year ago they had an affair, and when Rocco ended the relationship Rosalinda took an overdose. She lived,' Shayna said, when Emma drew a sharp breath, 'but she hasn't worked since her suicide attempt. She maintains that he promised her they had a future together, although I actually find that hard to believe,' Shayna admitted. 'Rocco is the archetypal playboy and his allergy to commitment is well known. But possibly he spun Rosalinda a line in order to bed her.'

Emma swallowed the bile that had risen in her throat. 'You're saying he deliberately misled her into believing he cared for her?'

Shayna gave another careless shrug. 'I don't know anything for sure. But, despite his apparent charm, Rocco has a ruthless streak. It's hardly surprising, I suppose, when he is the grandson of Silvio D'Angelo—one of the most powerful businessmen in Italy. You don't get to build a company the size of Eleganza by being a pussycat, that's for sure. And of course Rocco's parents were both utterly selfish. He told me once that witnessing their turbulent relationship had put him off marriage for life.'

Emma spent the rest of the evening chatting and smiling until her jaw ached, while carefully avoiding Rocco. His frustration was evident in his narrowed stare, but he was unable to challenge her when she stuck faithfully to his grandmother's side.

It was after eleven by the time the last guests departed and she escorted a weary but happy Cordelia up to bed.

'It was so nice to meet Rocco's friends, and so good of him to arrange the party. He has always had a kind heart.' The elderly lady sighed, her face suddenly sad. 'He had a hard time when he was a teenager. Giovanni's death was a tragic accident, but Rocco blamed himself.'

'Giovanni was only young when he died, wasn't he?' Emma murmured, busying herself with hanging Cordelia's dress in the wardrobe.

'Yes, poor boy. Gio was a demanding child. He was diagnosed with a mild form of autism and my daughter couldn't cope with him. I'm afraid she left Rocco in charge of him much too often.'

'What actually happened?' Emma could not contain her curiosity. 'How did Giovanni die?'

'The boys were staying at Nunstead Hall for the Christmas holidays. It was bitterly cold that winter, and the lake had frozen over,' Cordelia recalled. 'Gio had been told a dozen times not to walk on the ice, but small boys don't recognise danger. Rocco almost lost his own life trying to save his brother. The gardener had to drag him out of the freezing water and physically restrain him from trying to swim to Gio. Because it was too late,' she said sombrely. 'Gio must have fallen through the ice some while before Rocco spotted him, and he was already dead.'

'How terrible.' Emma shivered as she imagined the horrific circumstances of Rocco's brother's death.

'Yes. And I'm not sure Rocco has ever come to terms with what he sees as his failure to save Gio.' Cordelia had been rummaging in her handbag and now gave a frustrated sigh. 'Emma, dear, I think I must have left my reading glasses downstairs.'

'I'll fetch them for you.'

Emma was glad to have a few moments alone to marshal her thoughts. In the space of one evening she had heard two conflicting stories about Rocco. According to his ex-mistress he had fooled Rosalinda Barinelli into believing he wanted a long-term relationship with her, and then heartlessly dumped her when he had tired of her and broken her heart. But from Cordelia she had heard that Rocco had been prepared to sacrifice his own life while attempting to save his younger brother. Who was the real Rocco? she wondered. A cruel deceiver, or a brave hero?

Perhaps he was both—just as Jack had been. Her mind whirled with jumbled emotions as painful memories resurfaced. Her husband had lost his life while heroically saving children from a burning house. But at the time of his death she had discovered that he had cheated on her and lied to her throughout their marriage. How could she trust any man after Jack? she thought bitterly. How could she trust Rocco after what she had heard about him from Shayna Manzzini?

Cordelia's glasses case was on a coffee table in the sitting room. Smiling at the maid who was tidying the room, Emma picked it up and retraced her steps back to the door. Rocco's voice made her halt.

'Running away again, Emma?' he drawled as he strolled through from the conservatory.

The electric lamps had been switched off, and in the soft, flickering light cast by the burned-down candles he appeared big and dark, his face in shadow so that she could not see his expression. But something in his hard voice warned her he was not in a good mood.

'I came down to find Cordelia's glasses,' she explained, waving the case she was holding.

'Maria will take them to her.' He addressed the maid in Italian, and the girl immediately hurried over to take the case from Emma before scurrying from the room, shutting the door behind her.

'Can I get you a drink?' Rocco walked over to the bar and refilled his own brandy glass.

'No, thank you.' Her nerves were as taut as an overstrung bow now that she was alone with Rocco. 'I'm tired and I'd like to go to bed.'

He gave her a sardonic look. 'Yes, I'm sure you've had an exhausting day, sitting in the garden with Cordelia, but nevertheless I would like a progress report on my grandmother. How is the burn on her hand?'

'Healing well—it doesn't need to be kept covered now that the risk of infection has passed. And Cordelia says it's not nearly so painful.'

He nodded. 'And how would you assess her general health?'

'She seems much less frail, which I am sure is down to the fact that she is eating properly. One of my main concerns when she was living at Nunstead Hall was that she didn't bother to cook for herself and seemed to survive on toast and cups of tea. She really enjoyed the party,' Emma told him, recalling Cordelia's pleasure at the evening.

'Good.' He stared at her speculatively. 'And how about

you? Did *you* enjoy tonight?' He hesitated for a heartbeat. 'I noticed you had a long conversation with Shayna.'

She flushed. 'Yes…she was very informative.'

'I don't doubt it,' Rocco murmured dryly. He swore silently. Shayna was a first-class gossip, and he would lay a bet that she was responsible for the expression of stark vulnerability in Emma's eyes.

'She said that the two of you were once lovers.'

'I have never professed to be a monk,' he said quietly. 'And it was a long time ago.'

Emma shrugged, determined to retain her dignity. 'It's really of no interest to me.'

'No?' he challenged softly. 'That's not the impression I received before the party. I got the impression that you were *very* interested, *cara*.'

Her flush deepened, but she forced herself to hold his gaze. 'My conversation with Shayna was a timely reminder of what kind of a man you are.'

Rocco's face darkened at her scathing tone. 'Explain that remark. What kind of a man am I?'

'One who deliberately allowed Rosalinda Barinelli to think you cared for her, and then dumped her when you were bored with her, leaving her so distraught that she attempted to take her own life.'

Anger surged inside him and he fought the temptation to drive his fist into the wall. 'Shayna really did a hatchet job, didn't she?' He took a deep breath. 'My relationship with Rosalinda is no secret. Every tabloid voiced an opinion on my culpability for the terrible events that took place soon after our affair ended. But only a handful of people are aware of the truth. My closest friends—the people who really know me—never doubted me,' he said harshly.

He drained his glass, slammed it down on the counter

and strode across to the door without another glance in her direction.

Emma bit her lip, remembering how she had initially misjudged him and accused him of not caring about his grandmother. She had been wrong about him then—could she have jumped to the wrong conclusions again now?

'Rocco!'

His hand was on the door handle. For a moment she thought he was going to ignore her, but then he slowly turned his head.

'What?'

His savage expression was not encouraging. 'There are always two sides to a story,' she said huskily.

'Yet you chose to believe the words of a woman you had only just met rather than ask for my side.' His jaw hardened. 'I'm beginning to think that friendship between us is impossible—especially when you are determined to believe the worst of me.'

She thought of the loving care he gave his grandmother, his gentle patience with Holly and the kindness he had shown her, and she felt ashamed that she had acted as judge and jury without allowing him to give his version of events. Shayna's revelation that she and Rocco had once been lovers had caused a flame of white-hot jealousy to sear her insides. He was right; she *had* wanted to believe the worst of him. But her reason for doing so had been an attempt at self-protection and a way of fighting her growing feelings for him.

'I'm sorry.'

Rocco stared at her downbent head and fought to control his frustration. He wished he could pull her into his arms and kiss away the doubt and insecurity that darkened her eyes. Even greater was his wish that he knew who had put those emotions there.

'I met Rosalinda when I was on a business trip in Rome and saw her performing in a play at the Teatro Nazional. We were introduced at an after-show party and there was an immediate attraction between us,' he revealed honestly. 'She was beautiful, ambitious and appeared to be extremely self-confident. Acting was her life, she assured me. She wasn't looking for a long-term relationship while she developed her career. If I had thought for one minute that she hoped I would make a commitment to her I would never have become involved with her. But she seemed content with a casual affair, and even when I ended the relationship a few months later she did not appear unduly upset.'

Rocco's expression became grim. 'I was horrified when I received a phone call from Rosalinda's parents to inform me that she had taken an overdose, and that I was the reason why. I swear I gave her no cause to think I was in love with her. The closeness she believed existed between us was in her imagination only. Her parents were very understanding. They explained that she had previously been diagnosed with bi-polar disorder and was prone to periods of depression, and also that she had unrealistic expectations about relationships. Without my knowledge she had been planning our wedding—even to the extent of buying a wedding dress.'

He looked away from Emma, not wanting to see the disbelief and disgust he was sure would be in her eyes. 'If you want the truth, not a day goes by when I don't feel guilty about Rosalinda,' he said harshly. 'Maybe I missed the signs of her emotional fragility, or maybe somehow I unwittingly led her to believe that I had deeper feelings for her.'

'I doubt it,' Emma said quietly. 'Bi-polar disorder is a complicated issue, but even without that being a factor it's not uncommon for people who are in love to see what they want to see.' And conversely to ignore warning signs that a relationship was not as perfect as they wished, she acknowledged silently. She had made excuses for Jack throughout their marriage because she had wanted to believe that he loved her as much as she loved him. She, more than anyone, could understand how Rosalinda might have kidded herself that Rocco cared for her.

She did not doubt that he had told her the truth. His remorse at what had happened was obviously genuine. He had not deliberately deceived Rosalinda, and he had been honest with *her*. He had made it clear that he wanted a sexual relationship with her, but that was *all* he wanted.

Why not take what he was offering and enjoy a few weeks of fun? she debated. Lord knew, she needed it. But to make love with him, to experience the seductive pleasure of his hands and his mouth caressing her naked flesh, would mean relinquishing her hold on her self-control. The prospect filled her with fear. What if sex wasn't enough for her? What if she wanted more than he could give? He had the power to hurt her. Not physically—her instincts told her he would be a skilled and considerate lover—but he had already undermined her defences and she was afraid he posed a very real threat to her heart.

She stiffened when he walked towards her, struggling for composure while her treacherous body trembled with fierce sexual awareness.

Rocco wondered if she was aware that he could read each fleeting thought that crossed her features. She was a volatile mixture of emotions, and if he had any sense he would end his pursuit and walk away from her. But his much lauded common sense seemed to fly out of the window when he looked into her grey eyes that reminded him of storm clouds or woodsmoke, depending on her mood.

'How old were you when you met Jack?'

Emma frowned at the unexpected question. 'I was twenty, and midway through my nurse's training.'

'Did you have other relationships before him?'

'Not really. I dated a couple of boys from school, but I studied hard to achieve the necessary grades for university and didn't have much time for boyfriends. Why do you ask?'

'It has occurred to me that if you haven't dated since your husband's death, and you weren't involved with any other guys before you married, that only leaves Jack as the person responsible for your deep sense of mistrust.' His eyes narrowed on her suddenly tense face. 'But that doesn't make sense, because you have led me to believe that it was a marriage made in heaven. So what is the truth about your relationship with Jack Marchant, Emma?'

What good would it do to admit that her marriage had been far from ideal? she thought dully. It would simply show what a gullible fool she had been. Jack was dead and no longer had the power to hurt her. But his parents and Holly would be hurt if she ever revealed that he had not been the perfect husband everyone believed.

'I'm not prepared to discuss my marriage,' she said stiffly.

He studied her intently for several moments, but to her relief did not pursue the subject. 'That is, of course, your prerogative.' He walked across to the door and this time opened it before glancing back at her. 'I have a series of business meetings scheduled in various European cities and I'll be leaving early tomorrow morning. If you have any concerns about my grandmother while I'm away you can contact me on my mobile phone.'

Emma's heart lurched at the news that he was leaving the villa. She wanted to ask him when he would be back.

Did he have a mistress—more than one—who he intended to visit while he was away?

She masked her disappointment with a cool smile. 'Fine, but I don't suppose I'll need you.'

Rocco's eyes glittered. He was tempted to haul her into his arms and prove that her need to assuage the sexual frustration which simmered between them was as great as his. He did not doubt that she would respond to him. After a week of stolen glances and intense awareness smouldering below the surface of their polite exchanges, their desire for each other was at combustion point. One spark would set it aflame. But would it be fair to light the fuse, knowing that for him the beginning of an affair always signalled its end?

For the first time in his life he found that his desire to protect Emma was stronger than his urgent need to take her to bed. Even more astonishingly, he was actually contemplating a relationship with her that he could envisage lasting longer than a few weeks. *Dio*, how had an averagely pretty English nurse brought him to the point where he was considering abandoning his long-held principles of never getting emotionally involved with any woman?

He tore his eyes from her. *'Buonanotte,'* he bade her harshly before he strode out of the door.

'I'm going to stay with Nanna and Grandpa,' Holly told Rocco, her big grey eyes glowing with excitement.

'That sounds like fun, *piccola*.' He smiled at the little girl and glanced enquiringly at her mother.

'Jack's parents have a holiday home in Nice and have invited Holly to spend a few days with them,' Emma explained, relieved that her voice sounded normal and did not give away the fact that her heart was thumping.

The past week that Rocco had been away had seemed

interminable. She'd had no idea when he would return, and although he had phoned her twice, their conversations had been stilted and exclusively about his grandmother. The unexpected sight of him at the breakfast table this morning had sent the air rushing from her lungs. 'Peter and Alison are flying into Genoa tomorrow. They plan to hire a car, collect Holly and drive along the coast into France.'

'Can I go and tell Bobbo?' Holly asked, seeing the dog run across the lawn.

At Emma's nod the little girl slipped off her chair and ran out into the garden. 'How do you feel about her being away from you?' Rocco murmured, noting the faintly wistful expression on her face.

'Fine.' She smiled ruefully when he arched his brows disbelievingly. 'It's only for a few days, and she'll have a wonderful time. Jack's parents dote on her, and I know they'll take good care of her.'

A necessary part of motherhood was learning to let go. She had no doubt that Holly would love spending time with her grandparents, but being parted from her little daughter *was* going to be a wrench, Emma acknowledged with a sigh.

'Cordelia tells me she is going to spend today with Barbara and Andrew Harris.'

'Yes, she's upstairs getting ready, and I'm going to drive her there.'

'How about we take Holly to the beach? We'll take Cordelia to Rapallo and on the way back stop off at Santa Margherita. It's a pretty seaside resort, and she'll be able to make sandcastles to her heart's content.'

Emma's first instinct was to refuse. The wild burst of pleasure she had felt when she had walked into the dining room and discovered that Rocco was home was ample proof that he affected her way too much. While he'd been away she had made the decision that she could not risk becoming involved with him. But his lazy smile undermined her defences. In faded jeans and a cream shirt open at the throat to reveal an expanse of olive gold skin and a sprinkling of dark chest hairs, he was irresistibly sexy. What harm would it do to spend one day with him? she argued with herself. After all, it would be purely for Holly's benefit.

She set down her coffee cup and gave him a composed smile. 'That sounds nice. Holly will love it.'

So cool, Rocco mused, his amusement mixed with an unexpected feeling of tenderness. The pulse beating erratically at the base of her throat told him she was not sure of herself, or of him, and once again her tangible vulnerability tugged on his insides.

Palm trees stood at regular intervals along the esplanade at Santa Margherita Ligure, which was lined with bars, restaurants and *gelaterie*, shaded by colourful striped awnings. The sea was crystal-clear beneath a cloudless blue sky, but Holly was more interested in the long sandy beach, and could barely contain her impatience as Rocco parked the car and lifted her out of her child seat.

Emma opened the boot and gathered up a plastic bucket and spade, a rug to sit on, towels and a bag containing all the paraphernalia required for one small child.

Her lips twitched when Rocco murmured, 'I thought we were spending the day here, not a week.'

Their eyes met and held, before she quickly glanced away and took hold of Holly's hand.

'You go and set up camp, and I'll get coffees for us.'

She watched him stride away, his height making him easy to spot among the crowd ambling along the esplanade, enjoying a leisurely Saturday. Dragging her gaze from his broad shoulders, she smiled at her excited daughter. 'Let's get building castles.'

Holly needed no persuading, and played happily in the sand while Emma spread out the rug. The sun was warm enough for her to remove her jacket. Rocco had been right; she would have been uncomfortably hot in the jeans and sweatshirts she had brought from England. The white pedal-pushers and blue-and-white checked shirt she had chosen from the selection of clothes he had bought her were stylish and elegant, and had no doubt cost a fortune, she thought ruefully.

'Mummy—a shell.' Holly held out her hand to reveal her find. 'I'm going to look for more.'

'Stay close,' Emma instructed. She kept her eyes on her daughter, but Holly did not wander far before she started to dig a hole in the sand.

A gull soared overhead, mewing plaintively, and gentle waves lapped rhythmically on the shore. Heavenly, Emma mused, lifting her face to the sun. It was hard to believe that only a couple of weeks ago she'd had to dress in umpteen layers to keep warm in the wintry conditions affecting Northumberland.

She glanced down the beach and squinted against the sunshine when she did not immediately see Holly. A bright pink bucket and spade were lying on the sand, but the little girl was no longer digging. Frowning, Emma looked along the beach to the left and right, sure she would spot Holly's distinctive yellow T-shirt. But there was no sign of her.

'Holly?' Feeling a faint flutter of concern, Emma stared towards the sea. A group of children were playing on the shoreline, but her daughter was not with them. *'Holly!'*

'What's the matter?'

She swung round at the sound of Rocco's voice. 'I can't see Holly. She was here a minute ago…' Once again she scanned the horizon, panic edging towards fear when there was no sight of the child.

'I'll look for her. She can't have gone far.' Rocco took his mobile from his pocket. 'Keep your phone to hand and I'll ring you as soon as I find her.'

Emma continued to scan along the beach, gnawing on her lip until she tasted blood. With every second that passed her tension went up a notch, but she forced herself to keep calm. Any minute now Rocco would walk back along the sand with Holly on his shoulders, she assured herself.

She spotted him striding towards her—alone. Terror swept through her and she ran across the beach to meet him

'I can't see her,' he revealed tautly.

'Oh, my God!' Her legs felt like jelly, and she clung to him when he slid a supporting arm around her waist. 'She *must* be here. I only took my eyes off her for a moment.' Guilt surged through her and she covered her mouth with a trembling hand, as if to hold back the anguished cry building inside her. 'Rocco...' She stared at him wildly as he activated his phone. 'What are you doing?'

'Calling the police.'

'The police!' A cold hand of dread squeezed her heart as the seriousness of the situation hit her hard. 'She *must* be on the beach somewhere,' she cried frantically. 'She must be.' Tears burned her eyes and she brushed them away impatiently. She needed to think, to stay calm in a crisis. But she wasn't dealing with an accident in the A&E unit; her precious daughter had disappeared and a multitude of terrible scenarios were swirling in her mind.

'We need to report that Holly is missing,' Rocco told her.

The quiet authority in his voice and the way he firmly

assumed control calmed Emma a little, and she took a shuddering breath.

'Of course she's here somewhere,' he reassured her. 'But the more people we have looking for her, the quicker we'll find her.'

CHAPTER EIGHT

'It's my fault. I didn't watch her properly.' Tears streamed down Emma's face as her tight control on her emotions gave way. 'What if something's happened to her?' She glanced fearfully towards the sea. 'Or someone has taken her?' she could barely voice her worst nightmare.

The utter devastation in her eyes caused Rocco's heart to clench. He, better than most, understood what she must be feeling, he acknowledged grimly. The realisation that a child was missing, the desperate search... It was twenty years since his brother had disappeared in the grounds of Nunstead Hall, but the memory of the sick fear he'd felt as he had searched for Gio would always haunt him. *Madre de Dio*, please make the outcome be different this time, he prayed.

He cradled Emma's head between his hands and stared into her eyes. 'Stop blaming yourself—you are the most devoted mother I have ever met. We'll find Holly, I promise you, *cara*.'

The following forty minutes were the worst of Emma's life. Not even when she had been told of Jack's death, or learned from his mistress how he had betrayed her, had she felt such raw anguish. Waiting for news was sheer torture. But all she could do was stay on the beach, in case Holly wandered back to the place where they had been sitting. Meanwhile, Rocco had called the staff from the Villa Lucia to join the search as they would easily recognise the little girl.

Every tragic story she had read in the newspapers about missing children circled in Emma's mind. The idea that she might never see her daughter again was too unbearable to contemplate, and she dropped her head in her hands and gave a keening moan.

'Emma…'

Rocco's voice sounded from some distance away. But something in his tone… She lowered her hands—and felt as though her heart had exploded in her chest when she saw him striding along the esplanade, holding Holly in his arms.

'Thank God—*thank God*!' Tears blinded her and her legs would barely support her, but she forced them to move as she stumbled up the beach.

That evening, Rocco knocked on the door of Emma's room. 'Is she asleep?' he murmured as she emerged from Holly's bedroom and quietly closed the interconnecting door.

'Yes. I'm not surprised she's worn out after chasing Bobbo round the garden all afternoon,' she replied, forcing a bright tone. 'And she's excited about seeing her grand-parents tomorrow.'

She could not bring herself to refer to what had happened at the beach. Holly had eventually been found down by the harbour, where she had fallen asleep on a pile of fishing nets. Emma went cold at the thought that her daughter might have fallen into the deep water of the port and drowned. Thankfully, the little girl seemed unaffected by the drama of the morning, but they had cut short their beach trip and returned to the villa, where Emma had determinedly hidden the after-effects of her own shock and kept to Holly's normal routine.

'Are you still going to allow her to go to Nice with your in-laws?'

She nodded. 'I'd prefer not to let her out of my sight ever again, but it wouldn't be fair to disappoint her by cancelling the trip, and I've no doubt that Jack's parents will take great care of her.'

Without warning, her eyes filled with tears. All afternoon she had pushed thoughts of Holly's disappearance firmly to the back of her mind, but now agonising memories returned of the crippling fear and desperation she had felt. Earlier, a long soak in the bath had eased some of her tension, but the horror of losing her daughter was something she would never forget, and she sank down onto the bed, her shoulders shaking as sobs racked her.

'*Cara.*'

Rocco's deep voice sounded close to her ear. She felt his arms around her, felt him lift her, and she had no strength—either physically or mentally—to fight him.

It was some while before she finally brought her emotions under control. Feeling horribly self-conscious, she scrubbed her eyes with the tissues Rocco had pushed into her hand and lifted her head—to discover that he had carried her along the hall to his suite of rooms. They were in his private sitting room, a spacious room decorated in modern shades of taupe and cream. A door standing ajar led to his bedroom, where Emma could see a vast bed draped in burgundy silk.

'I thought you would not want to risk waking Holly,' he explained, correctly interpreting her questioning look.

Colour stained her cheeks at the thought of how she had broken down in front of him. 'I'm sorry,' she muttered, only now realising how close he was sitting next to her on the sofa. His arm was stretched along the back, and she had a horrible feeling that she had rested her head on his shoulder while she had been crying. She grimaced. 'I'm sure you have better things to do than put up with me snivelling all over you.'

'You've been through hell,' he said quietly. 'It's better not to bottle up your emotions.'

Something in his voice drew her gaze to his face, and her heart turned over at the haunted expression in his eyes. 'Is that what you did after your brother died?' she asked softly. 'Cordelia told me about Giovanni's accident.'

'Did my grandmother tell you that if I had looked after Gio properly there wouldn't have been an accident?' Rocco's jaw clenched. 'I can never escape the fact that my resentment at my mother leaving me to babysit yet again resulted in my brother's death. I failed Gio,' he said harshly. 'He wasn't an easy child, and he had a wild streak, but I loved him. He looked up to me and depended on me to look out for him. I will always live with the knowledge that I let him down.'

'You were a teenager—just a boy.' Her heart aching at his undisguised pain, Emma acted instinctively, leaning towards him and clasping his hand. 'Cordelia said that your parents should have taken more responsibility for Gio. You almost lost your life trying to save him all those years ago. And as for today…' Her voice broke. 'When I realised Holly was missing, I was so scared. I couldn't think. I didn't know what to do. But you took charge and organised the search. While I was stupidly panicking, you did everything you could to find her, and I…' She swallowed the lump in her throat and gave him a wobbly smile. 'I'm so glad you were there.'

Emotions were hell, she thought ruefully as tears once again blurred her vision. The terror of losing Holly had stripped away her protective shell, leaving her feeling painfully vulnerable. For the past three years she had brought up her daughter on her own, and even though it had been hard sometimes she felt proud that she had not needed help from anyone. But today she had needed Rocco. He had been her rock, she acknowledged, her heart swelling with the intensity of her feelings.

'What happened to your brother was a tragic accident,' she told him softly. 'You didn't fail him, and today you didn't fail Holly or me.'

Her words were like healing balm on a wound that was still raw so many years after Gio's death. For the first time since he was fifteen Rocco felt a sense of release from the guilt that had weighed heavily on him. Since the day he had cradled his brother's lifeless body in his arms he had felt frozen inside. He had avoided relationships where his emotions might be involved. It was easier that way—safer not to care.

But with Emma it was different. She had crept under his guard, and without knowing how or when it had happened he found that he was concerned for her well-being. When her daughter had gone missing he had felt her agony, and he would have moved heaven and earth to reunite her with Holly.

Emma caught her breath when Rocco curled his fingers around hers and lifted her hand to his mouth, to graze his lips across her knuckles. His golden tiger's eyes burned into hers and she became conscious of the subtle shift in the atmosphere between them. Moments before he had provided comfort and a sense of security, but now the tiny hairs on her body stood on end as she felt the tangible quiver of their mutual sexual awareness.

He moved his hand from the back of the sofa to her shoulder and gently propelled her towards him. In the thick silence she was sure he would hear her thudding heart, just as she heard the sudden quickening of his breath as he slanted his mouth over hers.

There was no thought in her head to deny him, and her lips trembled a little with the intensity of emotions unfurling inside her. Trust—something she had been certain she could never feel again—enfolded her as Rocco tightened his arms around her. His kiss was tender, evocative and it tugged on her heart. She felt safe with him—confident to relax her guard and allow him to discover the innately sensual nature that she had tried so hard to hide.

What was it about this woman that drove him to the brink with a single kiss? Rocco asked himself. He slid his fingers into the silky bell of hair that framed her face and accepted that the answer did not matter. The moist softness of her lips beneath his, the feel of her parting them to welcome the bold sweep of his tongue blew his mind and his hunger for her overwhelmed him.

Her skin felt like satin as he pressed his mouth to her throat and found the pulse beating erratically at its base. He pushed her peach-coloured silk robe aside and bared her shoulder to trace the fragile line of her collarbone. *Dio*, in his past he had had more women than he could count, and his reputation as a playboy was well deserved, but at this moment he felt like a youth again—barely able to control his surging hormones or prevent his hands from shaking as he undressed a woman for the first time.

Slowly, he drew the narrow strap of her negligee down her arm, revealing inch by delicious inch the creamy slope of her breast, and his breath hissed between his teeth when at last he cupped her naked flesh in his palm. Shaking with the strength of his desire, he lowered his head and flicked his tongue across her rosy-pink nipple, back and forth, until it hardened and he took the engorged peak fully into his mouth.

Emma could not restrain a soft cry of pleasure when Rocco suckled her breast. Sensation arced down her body and pooled between her legs. The slow build of passion changed to a feverish need that demanded appeasement, and a tremor of fierce hunger shot through her as he removed her robe and tugged her negligee down to her waist, baring both her breasts to his heated gaze.

When he laved first one nipple and then its twin she arched her back in mute supplication. Her body had never felt more alive than it did at that moment, every nerve-ending acutely sensitive as she trembled beneath the erotic onslaught wrought by his hands and mouth.

He covered her lips with his own once again, and this time the kiss was hot and urgent, their tongues locked in a sensual duel. Their breathing was ragged when at last he lifted his head and stared down at her, with feral hunger blazing in his eyes.

'*Ti volglio*—I want you,' he said, his voice rough with need.

Rocco had never felt like this before—never felt such an intensity of desire that filled every cell in his body and drove everything from his mind but his desperate longing to make love to Emma. From the very beginning he had felt a connection with her that even now he did not fully understand. She was his woman. He felt it in his blood, in his bones, deep down in the centre of his soul. She belonged to him and he *would* claim her.

'Yes.' The single word whispered from Emma's lips, as fragile as gossamer yet strong with certainty. She knew beyond doubt that she wanted Rocco to make love to her. The past, and the pain Jack had caused her, no longer mattered, and the future was tomorrow. She could only focus on the present and seize this moment with this man, who had edged stealthily into her heart.

She met his gaze steadily when he stood up and drew her to her feet. He tugged her negligee over her hips so that the slip of silk slithered to the floor, and then with heart-stopping deliberation hooked his fingers into the edge of her panties and pulled them slowly down. She watched the convulsive movement of his throat as he swallowed, saw the predatory hunger blazing in his eyes, and caught her breath when he slid his fingers into the triangle of red-gold curls between her legs.

'*Sei bella*, Emma,' he growled as he swept her up into his arms and strode into his bedroom. 'I have to have you now. Feel how much I want you,' he demanded raggedly, setting her on the edge of the bed and pressing her hand against the rock-hard bulge beneath his trousers.

Her eyes widened; excitement and a faint flutter of trepidation filling her as she stroked the burgeoning proof of his arousal. It had been a long time since she had had sex. Jack had been dead for over three years, and in the months prior to his death he had seemed to be put off by her changing shape due to pregnancy.

Memories of how hurt she had felt pierced her, but she refused to live in the past any more. She was no longer the naive girl who had been so overwhelmed by her handsome, charming husband that she had overlooked his many faults. At twenty-eight, she was a strong, independent woman, capable of making her own choices, and right now she chose to be with Rocco.

The fierce desire burning in his eyes restored her confidence in her body. Emboldened in a way she had never felt before, she gave him a demure smile. But her eyes gleamed wickedly as she undid his zip.

'You seem to be experiencing massive pressure, *signor*. As a nurse, I feel it is my duty to relieve your symptoms.'

'Witch.' He gave a hoarse laugh, driven to the edge by her teasing tone. Now was not a good time to discover she was a sex kitten, he thought self-derisively. He wanted this first time with her to be a long, sensual seduction, but he was so turned on that he feared he was about to explode, and his need to possess her took on a new urgency.

Barely able to control his impatience, he ripped off his shirt and dropped his trousers. He pulled his boxers down and shuddered as he imagined sheathing himself in the silken embrace of Emma's body. But the slight shadow of wariness in her eyes forced him to exert control over his rampant libido. He was sure she hadn't been with a man since her husband, and he knew he must slow the pace and ensure she was fully aroused before he possessed her.

With a flick of his wrist he pulled back the bedspread and lifted her into his arms, to settle her on the pillows before stretching out next to her and drawing her to him. The contrast of her pale limbs with his darkly tanned body was intensely erotic. Her skin was velvet-soft, where he was all hard muscle and sinew, and he delighted in the feel of her firm, rounded breasts pressing against his chest. He caught her faint sigh with his lips and initiated a slow, languorous kiss that became a sensual feast as he took it to another level that was unashamedly erotic.

Lost in the mastery of Rocco's kiss, Emma gave a little shiver of anticipation when he skimmed his hand over her stomach and continued a tantalising path down her body to slip between her thighs. She offered no resistance when he gently pushed her legs apart. Sexual excitement flooded her, and she caught her breath as she felt him delicately stroke the swollen lips of her vagina before he parted her and slid a finger into her.

A gasp escaped her when he proceeded to explore her with an expertise that swiftly brought her to the brink. He held her there, trembling and eager, and then, to her shock, replaced his fingers with his mouth.

'Rocco…'

He heard the uncertainty in her voice and lifted his head. 'Don't you like it?'

'I don't know,' she revealed honestly.

So the Superman husband had never given her the pleasure of oral sex? Rocco felt a spurt of surprise at the man's selfishness, quickly followed by a surge of masculine triumph that he would be the first to bestow that gift.

'Let me show you, *cara*,' he murmured, dipping his head once more and applying himself to his appointed task with a thoroughness that soon had her writhing beneath him. His own excitement mounted when he flicked his tongue across the tight bud of her clitoris and she gave a guttural cry.

'Please…' She had never been so fiercely aroused, so desperate for him to possess her and assuage the restless ache of longing deep in her pelvis. Rocco was a sorcerer, and she was utterly enslaved in his sensual spell.

'I intend to please you, *cara*,' he assured her thickly.

Emma was caught up in the maelstrom of incredible sensations he was creating. Her eyes flew open when she felt Rocco move away from her. He smiled at the disappointment in her eyes and handed her the protective sheath he had retrieved from the drawer in the bedside table.

'You put it on for me.'

Colour stained her cheeks. She was a nurse, for heaven's sake, and this was certainly not the first time she had seen the male form, Emma reminded herself. But the size of Rocco's erection took her breath away and she fumbled to open the packet. He was iron-hard beneath her fingertips as she eased the sheath over him. Dear heaven, would she be able to take him? she wondered, feeling a flicker of doubt.

Her heart was thudding beneath her ribs as he pushed her flat on her back and knelt over her, one hair-roughened thigh firmly nudging her legs apart. He kissed her mouth and then trailed his lips down her throat to her breasts, sucking on one taut peak and then the other, until she whimpered with an intensity of pleasure that was almost more than she could withstand.

Only then, when she was trembling with need, did he ease forward and penetrate her with a deep thrust, pausing for a moment while her internal muscles stretched to accommodate his solid length, before he withdrew a little and thrust again.

'Okay?' he asked softly, resting his forehead lightly on hers so that their eyelashes almost tangled.

Passion mixed with tenderness was a potent combination, she thought shakily. She felt connected to him in a far more fundamental way than simply the joining of their bodies, and his gentle consideration touched her heart.

'I'm okay as long as you promise not to stop doing that,' she murmured—*that* being another thrust, and then another. Each rhythmic stroke was taking her higher, so that within minutes she was hovering on the edge of some mystical place that she had absolute faith he would lead her into.

'I wish this could last for ever, *cara*,' Rocco groaned. 'But I have desired you for so long that I'm afraid you will have to forgive my impatience this time.' Driven beyond the limits of his control, he increased his pace and his strokes became faster, harder and so intense that Emma clung to his shoulders while the waves of sensation built to a crescendo.

The explosion was violent, and yet drenchingly sweet—

spasms of exquisite pleasure radiating from her central core in an orgasm that was more mind-blowing than anything she had ever experienced in her life. She felt boneless, mindless, and her eyelashes drifted down so that her entire being was focused on the instinctive clenching and unclenching of internal muscles.

'Look at me, Emma,' Rocco demanded, aware that he was fighting a losing battle with his control. A degree of male pride made him want to be sure that in the climax of passion she knew it was *him* she was making love with, not a ghost from the past.

She opened her eyes and stared into his glittering golden gaze. For a few seconds he stilled, his big body shaking with the effort of holding back the tide. But he could not fight its relentless force and threw back his head, a harsh groan torn from his throat as his control shattered and he experienced the ecstasy of release.

His convulsive shudders evoked a feeling of fierce tenderness in Emma. This strong, powerful man could be vulnerable in her arms. Instinctively she hugged him close, stroking her fingers through his hair and gently pressing her lips to his cheek. *This* was what making love should be, she thought softly. A complete union of two bodies in perfect accord.

But for her it had been so much more. She could no longer deny the truth to herself. Love had crept into her heart and ensnared her soul, and that was why she had given her body to Rocco. He had restored her self-belief and healed the hurt Jack had caused. Making love with Rocco had been the most profound experience of her life, one that she would never regret or forget, and the beauty of what they had shared brought tears to her eyes.

Rocco's chest heaved as he lay lax on top of Emma, aftershocks of pleasure still rippling through him. He felt relaxed and sated, and strangely reluctant to withdraw from her. For the first time in his life he had felt a union that went beyond the physical joining of two bodies. It was almost as if their souls had meshed.

He lifted his face from her neck and sought her mouth, but the dampness on her cheek made him stiffen. The realisation that she was crying felt like a knife in his ribs. Had making love with him brought back memories of the husband she still grieved for? *Did she wish he was Jack?*

The unwelcome idea brought him to his senses and he rolled off her. What had he been thinking? There was no special union between them. His soul was untouched, inviolate. The sex had been good—more than good— mind-blowing—but that was all it was. There was no reason to dress it up and look for things that didn't exist— emotions that he did not want.

He turned his head just as Emma hastily brushed her hand across her face. Clearly she did not want him to see her tears, and he did not want to know the reason for them.

She gave a tiny yawn and looked mortified. 'I'm sorry— it's been quite a day,' she said huskily. Reaction to the day's events, its happy outcome and spectacular conclusion, was hitting Emma hard, and she was struggling against the waves of tiredness that threatened to engulf her.

Rocco knew she was thinking of those endless minutes on the beach, when her daughter had been missing, and despite his determination to ban emotions from his relationship with her he felt a tug of compassion. She looked exhausted and infinitely fragile, her eyes huge and dark with shadows.

'Come,' he said gently, and he gathered her close.

His body immediately stirred once more as he traced his hands over her tempting curves, but he ignored the siren song of desire and gave in to a deeper need simply to hold her while she fell asleep in his arms.

Emma was already at the breakfast table when Rocco strode into the dining room the following morning. Her cool smile did nothing to allay the annoyance he'd felt when he had woken to find that she had left his bed some time during the night, but the flush of colour that stained her cheeks and the way she hastily looked away from him as he sat down opposite her gave him some measure of satisfaction. He was used to being in control of his relationships and usually *he* was the one to leave his mistress's bed. The role reversal had left him with a distinct sense of pique.

But everything with this woman was different, he acknowledged ruefully as he poured himself coffee from the jug, added a spoonful of sugar and took a sip of the strong black liquid. Emma had never played by the rules—which made her capitulation the previous night all the sweeter—but he was insulted that she had crept back to her own room like a thief in the night. Particularly as he had been painfully aroused when he had reached for her in the early hours. His body was still throbbing with sexual frustration. He was going to have to set a few ground rules and let her know that *he* would call the shots during their affair, he decided.

'Nanna and Grandpa are coming soon.' A high-pitched, childish voice drew him from his thoughts, and he smiled at Holly, who was wriggling on her seat, barely able to contain her impatience at the prospect of seeing her grandparents. 'Very soon—aren't they, Mummy?'

'Yes, but if you don't eat some breakfast you're going to be too hungry to go on a trip with them. Now, please eat some yogurt,' Emma said firmly.

Catching her eye, Rocco murmured, 'Someone is very excited.'

'You wouldn't believe,' came the rueful reply. 'I knew she would be up early, but we've read a whole book of fairy tales since five o'clock this morning.'

He felt himself relax as the reason for her departure from his bed became clear. Emma would always put her daughter beyond any other consideration, and he respected her for that. Unlike his own mother who, when he had been a child, had frequently entertained her lovers at the family home, and had not cared about his confusion when he had walked into her room and found her in bed with a man who was not his father.

His parents had *not* been good role models for marriage. His childhood had been punctuated by their rows and affairs, their dramatic reunions, followed inevitably by bitter separations. No wonder he had vowed to steer clear of the outdated institution of holy matrimony, he thought sardonically. Why would he choose to tie himself to one woman when he knew he would grow bored with a relationship within weeks?

But lately he had found himself equally bored with meaningless sexual encounters. He had been aware of a vague sense that there had to be something more. But then he'd remember his parents' vipers pit of a relationship and realise that love was an illusion—wasn't it?

He raked a hand through his hair and ignored the dish of freshly baked rolls the maid had placed on the table, finding that his appetite had disappeared. Why did a snippy English nurse make him suddenly question everything? he wondered irritably.

Being introduced to Emma's in-laws when they arrived half an hour later was an uncomfortable experience for Rocco, considering that he had just slept with their dead son's wife, but he exerted his usual easy charm and welcomed them to the Villa Lucia.

It was immediately clear that the Marchants adored their granddaughter and shared a close bond with Emma—and that they had been devastated by the death of their son.

'Jack was our only child,' Alison told Rocco, while Emma went to check that she had packed Holly's favourite soft toy. 'Holly lives on through him.' Tears filled her eyes, and her grief was painful to witness. 'Emma is a lovely girl. Peter and I hope she'll marry again one day, but of course Jack was the love of her life.'

'I understand,' Rocco murmured.

What he did not understand was why Emma shied away from ever talking about her husband, and why the mention of his name caused her to withdraw into herself. Mystery surrounded her relationship with Jack Marchant, and he felt frustrated that even though they had shared the most intense sexual experience last night she did not trust him enough to confide in him.

Determined not to risk upsetting Holly by indulging in an extended farewell, Emma kept a tight hold on her emotions as she leaned into the car and gave the little girl a kiss and a brief hug. 'Be good for Nanna and Grandpa, won't you?'

'I will, Mummy. Love you.'

Dear, sweet Holly. So trusting and innocent and infinitely precious. She would willingly lay down her life for her child, Emma acknowledged, blinking back tears as her parents-in-law's car with its precious cargo rounded a bend and disappeared from view.

'She'll be back in a few days,' Rocco reminded her.

'I know.' She forced a smile. 'I don't know what to do with myself now that Cordelia has accepted the Harrises' invitation to stay in Rapallo with them for a couple of days and Holly has gone. I think I might be bored.'

'Assuredly not, *cara*,' Rocco drawled, the velvet-soft sensuality in his voice sending a quiver down Emma's spine. 'I can think of a number of ways to keep you occupied.'

His eyes roamed over her and he congratulated himself on his excellent sense of taste in female attire. The short denim skirt he'd bought her when she had first arrived in Portofino moulded her pert derrière and revealed a tantalising amount of slender, lightly tanned thighs, while the simple white T-shirt clung to her generous breasts like a second skin. An erotic fantasy filled his mind, of stripping her right there on the front lawn and tumbling her down onto the sweet-scented camomile.

Reality intruded as he remembered the report on his desk that required his urgent attention, and the several hours of work waiting on his laptop.

The glimmer of tears clinging to her lower lashes like tiny raindrops caused him to abandon both ideas. Work could wait, and he would have to control his sexual frustration for a while. Emma was putting on a brave face, but he could see what a wrench she found it to be parted from her daughter. Once again he was surprised to find that the desire to comfort and protect her was stronger than his desire to satisfy his sexual urges.

He looped his arms around her waist and could not resist dropping a light kiss on her mouth, smiling lazily at her startled look and the flush of pink that stained her cheeks. Last night she had been a passionate temptress in his bed, and her shyness this morning both amused and touched him.

'I want to spend the day with you,' he said softly. 'How about we take my boat out? We can sail along the coast to Camogli and have lunch there.' He drew her closer, so that their bodies were pressed together and she could be in no doubt of his state of arousal. 'And afterwards we'll have a siesta onboard the *Anna-Maria*.'

Emma caught her breath at the hungry gleam in Rocco's eyes, and felt the sweet seduction of sexual anticipation unfurl in the pit of her stomach.

'You want to spend the afternoon sleeping?' she queried demurely.

His rough laugh could not disguise his rampant desire. 'Let me put it another way, *cara*. You will be lying down, but do not expect to get much rest.'

CHAPTER NINE

CAMOGLI was a pretty coastal village with a busy harbour, where sleek motor yachts were moored next to brightly painted fishing boats. Emma had enjoyed the leisurely trip there on board Rocco's twenty-foot cruiser, which was the epitome of luxury. It was a perfect day, with a cloudless blue sky and the sun shimmering on the crystal clear sea. As she had stood on the deck, with his arm around her waist and the breeze playing with her hair, she had felt that she had stepped into another world.

It was a million miles away from her life with Holly in Northumberland, but in a few short weeks she would leave Italy and Rocco, she reminded herself. She was determined not to be overwhelmed by this peek into a multimillionaire's lifestyle. But when she looked into his golden tiger's eyes and saw the predatory hunger in their depths it was hard not to feel overwhelmed by him.

Along the way they had stopped at a famous landmark on the Ligurian coast, San Fruttuoso, and had spent an hour exploring the beautiful Benedictine monastery there, which had been built on the beach.

Now they were sitting outside a charming harbourside restaurant in Camogli. Lunch had consisted of scallops, followed by the local dish *brazino in tegare*—sea bass cooked with white wine and tomatoes—served with a bottle of Pinot Grigio. The deliciously crisp white wine had induced a pleasant lethargy in Emma, and she ruefully acknowledged that she needed the cup of strong black coffee Rocco had ordered at the end of the meal.

Her heart flipped in her chest when she looked across the table at him. In black jeans and polo shirt, his eyes hidden behind designer shades and his silky dark hair falling across his brow, he looked devastatingly sexy. From the numerous female glances cast in his direction, she was not the only woman to find him so, she noted.

They had spent a pleasant few hours discussing everything from politics to the arts, and had discovered a shared taste for a new author of complex thrillers, but now Rocco leaned back in his chair and sipped his coffee before asking, 'Did you always want to be a nurse?'

The question provided a welcome distraction from her fierce awareness of him and Emma nodded. 'Yes—as far back as I can remember. I grew up on my parents' farm and for a while I thought about training to be a vet, but by the time I left school I knew that nursing was my vocation.'

'I imagine it's not always an easy job? There must be occasions, incidents which you find upsetting.' Rocco had witnessed her compassion in her treatment of his grandmother, and he suspected that beneath her guise of brisk and efficient nurse she had a heart as soft as butter.

'Sometimes,' she admitted. 'The death of a patient is always hard, but the rewards of the job far outweigh the negatives. After I'd completed my training I worked for six months in Liberia. The country has been torn apart by years of civil war, and medical facilities are primitive, to say the least. It was so sad to see people—especially children—dying from preventable illnesses such as malaria and measles. But the trip was an amazingly uplifting experience. The people have suffered so much, but they are determined to improve their lives, and it was good to know that I was helping them in some small way. When Holly is older I'd like to work in Africa again.'

'So, after Africa you returned to England, married Jack and lived happily until his tragic death?'

'Yes.' She avoided Rocco's speculative stare, unaware that the sparkle in her eyes had suddenly faded.

Her happiness had been built on the illusion that Jack had loved her as she had loved him, and it still hurt to think of all the times he had been unfaithful. Sometimes she wondered if it would have been better to have found out about his infidelity sooner, so that at least she could have confronted him about it. But he had died on the same day that his mistress had revealed his true nature, and Emma's grief had been mixed with anger and bitterness that he had betrayed her trust so cruelly.

'How about you?' she said, desperate to steer the conversation away from her marriage. 'Did you ever want to become an actor like your parents?'

'*Dio*, no!' Rocco's reply was swift and succinct. 'There was quite enough artistic temperament in the family with the two of them,' he said sardonically.

'Flora and Enrico's life had been a continuous performance,' he explained, 'and, like a Shakespearian tragedy, full of drama. Neither of them had been able to cope with Gio's behavioural problems, but when he'd died they had played the role of grief-stricken parents.'

'They did consider sending me to a performing arts school, but fortunately my grandfather intervened. My father had never had any interest in joining the family company, but Silvio was determined that I would be his heir and one day take over as head of Eleganza.'

'Didn't you mind having your future mapped out by

your grandfather?' Emma asked curiously, thinking that Silvio D'Angelo sounded a formidable character.

Rocco shook his head. 'It was my choice to study engineering at university. I am interested in all aspects of the motor industry, but the development side—thinking of new ideas and using new technologies—excites me the most. The project I'm involved with at the moment is to design a high-performance hybrid sports car which uses an electrically powered engine as well as an internal combustion engine that will result in a reduction in the use of fossil fuels.' He grinned, his enthusiasm making him seem suddenly boyish. 'I'm probably boring you,' he said ruefully. 'Most women get a glazed look in their eyes when I talk about my work.'

'No, I think it's fascinating,' Emma told him honestly. 'I guess I'm not like the other women.'

'That is an understatement, *cara*,' he assured her gravely.

No other woman had ever made him feel this way, Rocco brooded. He had had more mistresses than he cared to admit, but his interest in them had never extended outside the bedroom door. He worked in a predominantly male environment, and although he might flirt with women, and charm them, he rarely talked to them about things that mattered to him. It was a new experience to be with a woman he valued as a friend as well as a lover. The sense of companionship he felt with Emma was something he hoped would continue for a long time. Which meant what? he asked himself, frowning. Did he envisage his affair with her lasting for longer than the three months she had agreed to stay in Italy as his grandmother's nurse?

He studied her beautiful face, framed by her golden bell of hair, and realised that the answer to his question was an unequivocal yes. He could not imagine a time when he would not want her. He dropped his gaze to her firm, full breasts and desire jackknifed through him as he imagined stripping off her T-shirt and bra and cradling her luscious flesh in his hands.

'I think it's time for that siesta,' he drawled softly. 'Are you sleepy, *mia bellezza*?'

Emma's stomach lurched with anticipation at the blatant sensuality in Rocco's voice. She had enjoyed the boat trip, and lunch, but all day she had been conscious of the sexual tension simmering between them. The idea that very soon he would spread her beneath him and make love to her with a wild passion that matched her own caused a flood of sticky heat to pool between her legs.

She met his gaze and gave him a demure smile. 'No, I'm not a bit tired.'

Her teasing tone inflamed his libido. 'We have to get out of here now—before I give in to temptation and make love to you on the table,' he growled, jerking to his feet and hustling her out of the restaurant.

He held her hand and they ran along the quay back to where the *Anna-Maria* was moored. Laughing and breathless, they stumbled onboard, and within minutes Rocco was steering the boat out of the harbour.

'We'll drop anchor a little way out from the shore, where we won't be disturbed,' he said, pulling her to him and claiming her mouth in a fiercely passionate kiss that left Emma in no doubt of his hunger for her.

The ringtone of his mobile phone drove them apart.

'I'll have to take this, *cara*,' he muttered reluctantly, 'it's Silvio.'

He spoke to his grandfather in Italian for a few moments, then ended the call and switched off his phone, before scooping Emma up into his arms and heading purposefully down the steps to the lower deck.

'The old man called to remind me that he's hosting a dinner party at his home tomorrow night, for a number of prestigious clients as well as Eleganza's top executives. I've told him I'll be bringing a guest.'

'Me?' Emma gave him a worried look. 'But what will your grandfather think? I mean, strictly speaking, I'm your employee. If I go to the party with you, won't he suspect there's something going on between us?'

'I don't give a damn what Silvio or anyone else thinks,' Rocco told her thickly as they reached the master cabin and he dropped her onto the bed. 'I want you with me. And if you are my employee I hope you are going to obey my every command, *cara*. Something is undoubtedly going on between us, and it's time you took your clothes *off*.'

The desire blazing in his eyes made Emma feel like a wanton seductress, and with a confidence she would never have imagined herself possessing she pulled her T-shirt over her head and wriggled out of her skirt. Liquid heat coursed through her veins as she watched Rocco dispense with his own clothes to reveal the broad, bronzed chest covered with wiry dark hairs. Her eyes followed a path over his powerful abdominal muscles and hard thighs, and she caught her breath at the sight of his proudly erect penis. She reached behind her to undo her bra and then, oh, so slowly, slid the straps down her arms.

'So you want to tease, do you?' He laughed raggedly as he pulled her to the edge of the bed and whipped her bra from her fingers, curling his hands possessively around her breasts. 'Do you know what happens to naughty nurses who like to tease? They have to suffer being kissed over every inch of their body.'

He started with her nipples, flicking his tongue across each taut bud until she whimpered. He relented and took one pebble-hard peak and then the other fully into his mouth. By the time he had peeled off her panties and continued her punishment with the most intimate caress of all Emma was gasping and desperate for him to take her.

She reached for him, and felt him shudder when she stroked him. With a groan he quickly donned a protective sheath and positioned himself between her thighs.

'Playtime's over, *cara*,' he growled, and he entered her with one deep thrust that filled her and gave her a sense of completeness that tugged on her heart.

Her man, her master. She welcomed each subsequent stroke and wrapped her legs around his back to increase the exquisite sensations that were building deep in her pelvis. The feeling of oneness she had with Rocco was like nothing she had ever experienced. It was as if their souls as well as their bodies had become a single entity: a circle that had no beginning and no end.

But there had to be an end, and it came in an explosive orgasm that caused her to rake her nails across his shoulders while her body pulsed with spasm after spasm of pleasure. He continued to drive into her, sending her over the edge for a second time, and as she tumbled he fell with her, uttering a savage groan in the ecstasy of their simultaneous release.

Afterward, Rocco settled her head on his shoulder and smiled when he saw her lashes flutter down to fan against her flushed cheeks. He would allow her a short siesta before he enjoyed her delectable body for a second time, and no doubt a third. He could not resist her, he acknowledged ruefully. But it was just good sex. He did not want a long-term relationship when experience had shown him that it might end in bitterness and acrimony, like his parents' hellish marriage and the marriages of so many of his contemporaries. But neither did he want to let her go, taunted a voice inside his head. At some point he was going to have to make a decision about where his affair with Emma would lead.

The following evening Rocco knocked on the door of Emma's bedroom, where she had gone to change for his grandfather's dinner party.

'Are you ready, *cara*?'

She spun round to face him, and he saw from her taut expression and the way she was twisting her hands together that she was as tense as a coiled spring.

'Just about. But, Rocco, I really don't think I should go with you. For one thing, Cordelia is tired after her trip to Rapallo—I think visiting three museums was a bit much for her. She seemed very frail when I collected her this afternoon, and I think I should stay here in case she needs me.'

'I've just been with Nonna, and she is delighted that you are going out for the evening.' He dismissed her argument. 'She says she's going to have an early night. And Beatrice is on hand should she require assistance.' He strolled across the room and slid his hand beneath her chin to tilt her face to his. 'What's the real issue here, Emma?'

'I won't fit in with your prestigious clients and top executives,' she mumbled. 'I'm not a glamorous socialite and I don't have anything interesting to say.'

Rocco gave her a quizzical look. 'You are the most interesting person I've ever met, and you have so much to say that is worthwhile. I would happily spend all evening talking with you rather than being bored to death by so-called "glamorous socialites", whose conversation is limited to gossip about celebrities or fashion.' He gave her an amused smile. 'You're one of the few women I know who fully understands the workings of the internal combustion engine.'

'I told you—I used to help my brother fix the farm tractors. But my experience as a grease-monkey is not an ideal topic for discussion at a posh dinner party,' she said dryly.

'You'll be fine, I promise. Silvio is looking forward to meeting you. And as for fitting in—in that dress you look elegant and sophisticated.' He ran his eyes over the floor-length black jersey-silk dress that moulded her curves and emphasised her slim waist. His voice thickened. 'And indescribably beautiful.'

Emma caught her breath at the sudden flare of emotion she glimpsed in his eyes, but it was gone before she could decipher it—hidden beneath the sweep of his dark lashes. In a black tuxedo and brilliant white shirt he looked mouth-wateringly sexy. She felt her heart rate quicken and gave a wry smile.

'So do you. Thank you for the flowers, by the way. They were a lovely surprise.' Her eyes lingered on the three dozen red roses that had been delivered to the villa during the day and were now arranged in a vase on her dressing table. Red roses were for love, she thought wistfully. But Rocco did not love her, and from all she had learned of him he would never give his heart to any woman.

'It's time to leave.'

His velvety voice drew her from her confused thoughts. Enjoy the present, and stop worrying about the future, she told herself as she slipped her hand in his and allowed him to lead her from the room.

'What do you think of my house, Mrs Marchant?'

Emma was standing by the window, gazing out at the night-time view of the city of Genoa, where graceful old buildings were illuminated by the golden glow emitted from the street lamps. She turned her head at the sound of the heavily accented voice to find that Silvio D'Angelo had joined her.

'It's incredible,' she replied honestly, recalling the tour Rocco had given her earlier of the five-storey house, whose elegant rooms were filled with priceless antiques. 'It's such a beautiful, historical building—as are so many of the other houses nearby.'

'This part of Genoa is known as the Old City, and is included on the World Heritage list,' Silvio told her.

Shorter and stockier than his grandson, he had a wrinkled face and grey hair that indicated that he must be well into his eighties, but there was a shrewd gleam in his dark eyes that Emma found unnerving.

She smiled hesitantly. 'Please—call me Emma.'

He dipped his head in acknowledgement. 'Rocco tells me you are a good friend of his?'

She felt herself blush. *Just good friends* was hardly an apt description of their relationship, she mused, recalling the numerous times he had made love to her the previous night. 'Yes. I'm staying at the Villa Lucia for a few weeks to act as a companion to Cordelia.'

Silvio's beady eyes seemed to bore into her. 'And after that you will return to England?'

Her stomach swooped at the prospect, but she hid her dismay and nodded. 'I'll be going back to my job as a district nurse.'

Her eyes were drawn across the room to where Rocco was chatting to a stunningly attractive woman who he had introduced earlier as Valentina Rosseti—the only female engineer on Eleganza's design team. From the way Valentina was batting her eyelashes at him she would lay a bet that the Italian woman wasn't thinking about hybrid engines now, Emma thought sourly.

Silvio followed her gaze and his expression became speculative. 'I am an old man,' he announced. 'I was ninety years old last month, and it is time I handed over control of Eleganza to my grandson.' He sighed heavily. 'But I have stipulated that Rocco must curb his playboy lifestyle before I assign full power of the company to him. He needs to marry a good Italian girl, and produce an heir to one day succeed him.'

Emma gave him a doubtful look. 'I don't think marriage is on Rocco's agenda.'

The elderly man snorted. 'My grandson knows his duty. Eleganza is his favourite mistress, and he will do whatever is required of him to take control of the company he loves.'

A gong sounded to call them to dinner, but her conversation with Silvio had unsettled Emma and she was unable to enjoy the five superb courses, each served with a different wine specially chosen to complement the food. It did not help that Rocco was seated at the far end of the table with his grandfather, Tino Manzzini and several of Eleganza's clients—presumably so that they could discuss business. Emma was seated next to one of Rocco's elderly uncles, who spoke little English, while to her other side was Shayna Manzzini.

'So Rocco decided to forgo his pretty young neighbour in favour of you,' the Canadian woman drawled towards the end of the meal, pushing away her dessert of Tiramisu untouched.

Emma had noted that she had barely eaten any dinner, and guessed that semi-starvation was how Shayna retained her model's figure. She was unsure how to respond to the comment, but Shayna did not seem to be waiting for a reply.

'I noticed at his grandmother's party that you couldn't take your eyes off him. But you do know it won't last, honey? Rocco doesn't do commitment.' She paused to ensure she had Emma's full attention and then said softly, 'Not even with the mother of his child.'

Trying to hide the fact that her hand was shaking, Emma put down her spoon, telling herself that it was the rich confection of mascarpone and cream in front of her that had made her feel sick. She had previous experience of Shayna's spiteful tongue, and was not inclined to believe a word she said. There was a lot of truth in the saying that hell knew no fury like a woman scorned, she thought wryly. But something in her expression must have revealed her uncertainty to Rocco's ex-mistress.

'I assume from your stricken look that he hasn't told you?' The model shrugged. 'Well, I'll grant you it is speculation rather than fact.'

'What is?' Emma demanded bluntly.

'That Rocco has a son by one of his mistresses. Rumour has it that the boy and his mother live here in Genoa, and that Rocco visits them every week. I guess that would explain why, according to my husband, no one can contact Eleganza's CEO after he leaves the office at midday every Friday.'

'There could be a dozen reasons why Rocco leaves work early,' Emma said tersely. In the past she had jumped to conclusions about him far too quickly and, as it had turned out, wrongly. She did not intend to make the same mistake again—especially at the words of an embittered woman who had had an affair with him years ago and clearly still resented the fact that he had dumped her.

She trusted Rocco.

The realisation settled like a warm glow around her heart. After having had her faith destroyed by Jack, she had never thought she would trust anyone ever again. But Rocco had always been honest with her—even to admitting that he did not want a long-term relationship. She had gone into their affair fully aware that it had no future, but she had no regrets. She would always treasure the time she had spent with him, she thought softly, conscious of the dull ache inside her when she envisaged returning to England without him. Her life would be a lot easier if she had not fallen in love with him, but that was her fault—not his.

'Rumours rarely amount to more than spiteful gossip,' she told Shayna coldly. 'And I certainly don't believe that Rocco has a secret child.' She thought of his gentle patience with her daughter, and was certain that if he ever had a child of his own he would be a devoted father. 'He's an honourable man.'

The model arched her finely plucked brows. 'Oh, dear, you're in love with him,' she drawled mockingly. 'Well, don't say I didn't warn you.'

Dinner finished soon after, and Emma managed to avoid Shayna for the rest of the party, but she was relieved when the evening drew to an end and Rocco escorted her out to his car. Doubts were like weeds, she thought dismally. They started out as a tiny seed but grew to smother rational thought as swiftly as Japanese knotweed left unchecked in a herbaceous border.

'You're very quiet, *cara*,' Rocco commented some twenty minutes later, as he turned the car onto the driveway in front of the Villa Lucia. He walked round to open the passenger door, frowning at her obvious reluctance to meet his gaze. 'Is anything wrong?'

'No,' Emma denied quickly. 'I was just thinking…about

things.' She hesitated, her heart drumming a warning tattoo beneath her ribs.

During her marriage she had never confronted Jack on the many occasions when he had arrived home from work hours later than she had been expecting him. The idea that he was seeing someone behind her back had hovered in her mind, but she had been scared to demand the truth and had pushed her suspicions away. Looking back, she regretted her lack of courage, and it made her determined to face problems head-on now.

She followed Rocco into the villa, but when he moved to draw her into his arms she stepped back from him, knowing that if he kissed her she would be lost. Sensing his frustration, she blurted out, 'Do you have any children?'

He stiffened, clearly shocked, and his eyes narrowed on her tense face. '*Dio*! What kind of question is that?' he demanded harshly. 'Of course I don't.'

'You admit that you have had numerous affairs,' Emma pushed on doggedly, despite his deepening frown. 'Surely it's possible that a woman from one of your past relationships could have given birth to your child?'

'No—it isn't,' Rocco told her curtly. 'I'm always careful, and there has never been any chance of an accidental pregnancy. What kind of a man do you think I am?' He gave a bitter laugh. 'On second thoughts, don't answer that. Past experience tells me that your reply won't be complimentary.'

He sounded hurt, Emma realised guiltily. His startled reaction had convinced her that she had made a big mistake in allowing Shayna's spiteful comments to take hold in her mind. She bit her lip. 'It was just a stupid thought,' she mumbled. 'Please forget I ever mentioned it.'

Rocco stared at her downcast face and was torn between wanting to shake some sense into her and kiss her senseless. '*If* I was a father, I would not be involved with you. I would be married to the mother of my child.'

Now it was her turn to look startled. 'I thought you didn't believe in marriage?'

'I admit that my parents' marriage was not a good advertisement. But a child's needs must take first priority, and although it might be old-fashioned I believe that children should grow up in a family unit with both their parents. Even though my mother and father argued frequently, I still had the sense that we were a family. When they split up I felt torn between them, and I wished they would get back together.'

The silence that fell prickled with tension. Certain that she had angered Rocco, and feeling uncertain of his mood, Emma studied the marble-tiled floor with apparent fascination.

'Let me ask *you* a question,' he said brusquely. 'Why don't you ever want to talk about Jack? I know you loved him,' he continued before she could reply, 'but it has been three years, and you can't keep your emotions locked away for ever.'

'What do you know of emotions?' she countered shakily. 'You're a playboy whose tally of ex-mistresses probably equals a cricket score. From the outset you've made it clear that our affair will be purely physical, and emotions will play no part in it.'

'Yes, I have,' Rocco agreed broodingly. 'And I was sure I meant it.' He stretched out his hand to tuck a lock of strawberry-blonde hair behind her ear and stared into her stormy grey eyes. 'Now I am not certain that my emotions are in my control. You have undermined the rules I have lived by all my adult life. I've discovered that I want a proper relationship with you, Emma,' he said softly, his smile a little rueful when she seemed to be struck dumb by his revelation.

Emma snatched a breath and tried desperately to steady her racing heart, but the expression in Rocco's eyes—a mixture of tenderness and sultry promise—was scrambling her brain. 'What kind of relationship?' she queried cautiously.

'One that involves us getting to know each other properly and sharing our thoughts…and feelings. I know there is Holly to consider, and that is why I think we should take things gradually, but I want you in my life, *cara*,' he said deeply.

He could no longer deny the truth to himself or to Emma. No other woman had ever made him feel this level of need, and with a muttered oath he pulled her into his arms. 'Is it so hard for you to trust me? I swear I don't want to hurt you. I'm prepared to take things one step at a time, but I need you to take that first step with me.' His voice dropped lower, his accent very pronounced as emotions he had never experienced before churned inside him. 'Will you, Emma?'

His face was so close to hers that his warm breath feathered across her lips, and she shook with longing for him to kiss her and seduce her with his sensual mastery. She had decided tonight, when she had chosen not to believe Shayna Manzzini's scurrilous accusations, that she *did* trust him, and she felt empowered that she had thrown off the shackles of her past.

'Yes,' she whispered, parting her lips eagerly beneath the pressure of his as he claimed her mouth in a kiss of pure possession.

CHAPTER TEN

SUNLIGHT slanting across her eyelids roused Emma from a deep sleep. She stretched, and smiled when a muscular arm immediately tightened around her. Cocooned in the relaxed state that preceded full wakefulness, she felt safe and totally secure, and her mouth curved into a soft smile when she lifted her lashes and met an enigmatic golden gaze.

'*Buongiorno, cara.*' Rocco brushed a kiss as light as thistledown over her lips.

'Were you watching me sleeping?' She could not disguise the faint note of vulnerability in her voice at the thought.

'It's a special part of my day—waking with you in my arms,' Rocco told her seriously. He traced the shape of her breasts and felt his body stir when her nipples hardened at his touch. 'Of course there are many other special moments,' he murmured huskily.

Emma caught her breath when he lowered his head and replaced his hands with his mouth, liquid heat pooling between her legs as he continued an erotic path across her stomach and down to tease the sensitive nub of her clitoris with his tongue. What followed was a slow, sensual loving that tugged on her soul as he positioned himself above her and entered her with exquisite care. His eyes locked with hers as he brought her to a shattering orgasm, and when their passion was finally spent he cradled her in his arms while their thundering hearts resumed a steady beat.

'I know why you're smiling,' Rocco said lazily, feeling a hand squeeze his heart as he studied her beautiful face. The silky bell of golden hair framed her flushed cheeks, and he thought that she had never looked lovelier. 'Holly is coming back today, isn't she?'

'Yes.' Emma had never imagined she could feel this happy. The past week that she and Rocco had been lovers had been filled with laughter and incredible passion, but she had missed her little daughter and ached to lift Holly into her arms and hug her close. 'Peter and Alison are flying home to England today, so I've arranged to meet them in Genoa. It's approximately a hundred-mile drive from Nice, so they should arrive about lunchtime.'

Unable to resist, she ran her hand lightly over his cheek, feeling the faint abrasion of stubble on his jaw. He was heart-stoppingly sexy first thing in the morning, she thought, feeling her stomach dip. 'You're welcome to join us for lunch.'

Rocco hesitated, thinking of the text message he had received from his half-brother a few moments before Emma had woken up: *See you after school today?*

It was the first time Marco had ever contacted him, and sensing the uncertainty behind the message Rocco had immediately texted back: *Of course.* The little boy was finally starting to trust him, and he could not let him down, he acknowledged heavily.

'I'd love to, *cara*, but I have an important appointment this afternoon. Tell Holly I'll see her when I get home from work tonight.' He glanced at his watch and threw back the sheet. 'Talking of work, my little temptress, I need to get moving. Fridays are always busy.'

He headed into the en-suite bathroom, and moments

later Emma heard the sound of the power shower. She tried to quash her disappointment that he could not meet them for lunch, reminding herself that he was the CEO of one of the biggest companies in Italy and could not rearrange his busy schedule for her.

Unbidden, Shayna Manzzini's comments slid insidiously into her head. *Rumour has it that the boy and his mother live here in Genoa, and that Rocco visits them every week.*

Rubbish, she thought firmly. Shayna was a nasty piece of work, and the rumour was nothing more than sheer bitchiness resulting from jealousy because the Canadian woman had realised that Emma and Rocco were lovers. Rocco had always been honest with her, and she felt confident that she could trust him. Yes, he had a reputation as a playboy, but he had stated that he wanted a meaningful relationship with her. He was not Jack, and it was not in his nature to deceive her.

Rocco stood beneath the powerful jet of water and tried to marshal his chaotic thoughts. Secrets were hell—and this wasn't even *his* secret, he brooded grimly. He wished he could tell Silvio about Marco. The old man was much stronger than a few months ago, when he had undergone major heart surgery. Back then the doctors had advised that he should not be subjected to any shocks, and telling him that he had an illegitimate grandson had been out of the question.

But the ultimate decision about whether he wanted to be part of the D'Angelo family had to be Marco's. Rocco had given his half-brother his word that he would tell no one of his true identity until Marco wanted it to be known. The little boy was coming round to the idea of meeting his grandfather, but until he made that choice Rocco felt he could not reveal the truth to anyone.

Damn Enrico for dumping this on him, Rocco thought bitterly. It was typical that he had been left to sort out the mess his father had left behind. He desperately wanted to confide in Emma, but he had worked hard to gain Marco's trust and he owed his little brother his loyalty. He could not break the promise he had made to a seven year-old child.

Reaching for a towel, Rocco rubbed his hair vigorously. There were a lot of things he wanted to tell Emma, he acknowledged, feeling his stomach clench with a nervous tension that was completely alien to him. He did not do nerves, or emotions, but both were churning in his gut—along with a feeling of vulnerability that he had never experienced before. All were the fault of an attractive English nurse with cool grey eyes and a smile that made his heart miss a beat.

So what was he going to do about it? he queried self-derisively. The situation demanded decisive action, but the possibility that for the first time in his life he might fail to achieve what he desired caused the cramping feeling in his stomach to intensify.

'Are we lost, Mummy?'

Emma glanced over her shoulder at Holly, who was sitting in her child seat in the back of the car, and gave what she hoped was a confident smile.

'Only a little bit, munchkin. I've stopped for a few minutes so that I can look at the map.'

The journey from Portofino to Genoa this morning had been relatively simple, and once she had left the main coast road and entered the city she had found the restaurant where she had arranged to meet her in-laws without any trouble. Trying to negotiate her way out of town, however, was proving more difficult. The roads were busy with Friday afternoon traffic, and although she felt reasonably confident driving on the right side of the road rather than the left, as was the law in England, she had been concentrating so hard on the flow of cars at a roundabout that she had missed the correct exit and ended up in a maze of narrow backstreets.

Map-reading had never been one of her strengths, Emma acknowledged with a sigh. She was tempted to ask for directions, but there were few people around, and her inability to speak Italian was likely to be a major stumbling block.

'Mummy, I'm hot.'

With the car's engine off, the lack of air-conditioning meant that the temperature inside the car was rising rapidly. Emma rubbed her brow, feeling the beginning of a headache. 'Okay,' she reassured Holly, 'we'll be moving in a minute.'

At the far end of the street a couple accompanied by a child riding a bike came into view. The gods might be kind and they would be able to speak English, she hoped, releasing her seat belt as the people drew nearer.

They were a striking couple, both tall—the man dark-haired and swarthy, the woman slender and elegant, with a mane of long platinum-blonde hair that suggested she was not a native Italian. Something about the man—his natural grace and air of supreme self-confidence—seemed curiously familiar. Frowning, Emma focused on the child—a boy of perhaps seven or eight years old—and her heart suddenly froze. The jet-black hair was not unusual for an Italian, but the perfect symmetry of his features, his eye-catching handsomeness even at a young age, bore an incredible resemblance to Rocco.

Don't be ridiculous, she told herself impatiently, angry for allowing the shadow of Shayna Manzzini's spite to hang over her. She was no longer the woman she had been after Jack's death, lacking in self-worth and terrified to trust her own judgement. She did not believe for one second that Rocco had a secret love child. But she could not tear her gaze from the boy on the bike. He was close to where she was parked now, and she saw that his eyes were an unusual amber colour—like tiger's eyes.

Bile rose in her throat, so acrid that she almost gagged. She felt as though she had been turned to stone and she watched, unable to move, as the boy leapt from his bike, stood it carefully against the wall and then hurtled back to the man who was drawing ever nearer. The man swung the boy high in the air, and they both laughed while the beautiful blonde woman looked on and smiled. The bond between the three of them was unmistakable—and now that he was close to the car so was the identity of the boy's father.

'Are we going now?'

'Yes, right now.' Spurred into action, Emma dragged her seat belt across her. She was terrified that Holly would spot Rocco, or that he would glance into the car. Why didn't she step out onto the pavement and confront him, as she should have done with Jack all those times when he'd arrived home late? a voice in her head demanded. The stark answer felt like a knife in her heart. It was because now, as during her marriage, she could not face the truth and see her pathetic dreams crumble to dust, she thought despairingly.

She had trusted Rocco. Dear heaven. She gave a bitter laugh. Had her blind faith in Jack taught her nothing? She had fallen in love with a playboy once and been cruelly betrayed. What kind of a fool was she to have made the exact same mistake a second time?

She started the engine and the sound drew the attention of the group on the pavement. Like a petrified rabbit caught in car headlights she stared at Rocco and saw him stiffen, watched the startled expression on his face turn to a frown. He took a step towards her and her instinct to flee kicked in. There was a horrible grinding noise as she clumsily selected a gear and the car shot down the road. She determinedly avoided looking into her rearview mirror for one last glimpse of Rocco, focused only on getting away from him.

Rocco gunned his sports car up the hill towards the Villa Lucia. The powerful V8 engine had eaten up the miles to Portofino, but it had been several hours since he had watched Emma race away down the road in Genoa and he was impatient to talk to her. Why had she shot off like that this afternoon? he brooded. He realised she must have been as surprised to see him as he had been to see her, and he did not understand why she had been in that part of the city. Recalling her tense face, he could not shake off a sense of grim foreboding.

It had turned out to be one hell of a day, he thought wearily. The new bike he had presented to Marco had finally won the little boy over. He had been shocked by the strong emotions that had surged through him when his half-brother had hugged him for the first time. It had brought back painful memories of Gio, and reinforced his determination to act as a father figure to Marco.

Emma's unexpected appearance and the disturbing, almost devastated expression he had glimpsed on her face had made him want to rush back to Portofino immediately. But Marco had fallen off the bike, and their subsequent trip to the hospital where he had been diagnosed with mild concussion meant that Rocco had been delayed in the city. Inga, Marco's mother, had been badly shaken by the accident, and even when Rocco had been assured that his brother would be fine he had felt duty-bound to stick around until Marco had been discharged.

At least Silvio had taken the news of his grandson better than expected. Marco had decided that he wanted to meet his grandfather, and Rocco had gone straight from the hospital to Silvio's house, to explain about the little boy. The old man had been shocked, and clearly dismayed that Enrico had kept his illegitimate son a secret for seven years. But Silvio was eager to meet Marco, and had agreed with Rocco that he should inherit a share of Eleganza.

Now, finally, he was free to tell Emma everything that was in his heart. Tension coiled in Rocco's gut and he gave a ragged laugh beneath his breath. Nerves were hell, and a new experience for him where a woman was concerned. But he had long ago realised that Emma was unique. He could only pray she shared his hopes for the future.

The discovery of a taxi parked outside the villa was puzzling. He drew up next to it just as Emma ran down the front steps with a suitcase in her hand. She stopped dead at the sight of him, and even from a distance of a few feet away Rocco could sense her tension.

She jerked back to life and threw the case into the boot of the taxi.

'What are you doing?' Emerging from his car, Rocco glanced into the taxi and saw Holly strapped into a child seat. The ominous feeling that his life was about to come crashing down intensified.

'Leaving,' Emma told him shortly.

Instinct warned him that her emotions were balanced on a knife-edge, and he resisted the temptation to grab her shoulders and demand to know what the hell was going on. 'I guessed that. But why? Your contract to work as Cordelia's private nurse is for three months.'

'Your grandmother no longer needs a nurse.' By a huge

effort of will Emma managed to keep her voice normal, hiding the fact that inside she was falling apart. Fate had a cruel sense of humour, she thought bitterly. If Rocco had arrived home five minutes later she would have already left, and been spared a confrontation with him.

Something was very wrong, Rocco realised. *'Cara...'* He took a step towards her, a hand outstretched.

'Don't,' she said violently, backing away from him. Her self-control cracked. 'Don't come near me.'

'Madre de Dio! What is going on, Emma?' Realising that she was about to climb into the taxi, Rocco caught hold of her arm and felt the tremor that ran through her.

'How can you ask me what's wrong?' she demanded, keeping her voice low for fear of upsetting Holly. 'I saw you today—*with your son.*'

Shock slowly turned to something cold and hard, like a lead weight in the pit of Rocco's stomach. When Emma snatched her arm out of his grasp he did not attempt to stop her. 'My *son*?'

'That boy you were with. Don't try to deny it,' Emma said wildly. 'Shayna told me about the rumour that you have a son by one of your mistresses and you visit them regularly.'

Nausea swept through her when she pictured the stunning blonde woman who had been with Rocco and the little boy. She had spent the past few hours thinking about it, and it all made perfect sense. Rocco knew his grandfather would not sign over full control of Eleganza to him unless he married an Italian woman, and so he had kept the fact that he had a son by his Nordic-looking mistress a secret. What other explanation could there be?

The dangerous gleam in Rocco's eyes sent a shiver through her. 'Naturally you would believe Shayna—

despite previous proof that she's a spiteful bitch,' he said sarcastically.

Stung by his icy disdain, she said fiercely, 'I didn't believe her at your grandfather's party. I trusted you. But you lied to me.' She held up her hand when he made to speak. 'You let me think that your afternoon's appointment was work-related, and that was why you couldn't meet me in Genoa. But I've seen the evidence that you were lying. The little boy you were with is the image of you.'

'So was Gio,' Rocco said harshly.

She frowned. 'What has that got to do with anything?'

'Think about it.'

She shook her head and reached once more for the taxi door. 'I don't want to think about anything. I just want to go.' Before the tears that felt like acid burning her eyes fell and he witnessed her utter devastation.

It would take a matter of minutes to explain about Marco—although whether Emma would believe him was open to question, Rocco thought grimly. Anger surged through him. If she had any faith in him he should not have to defend himself. Her readiness to believe Shayna proved that she had never trusted him.

She pulled open the car door and he felt a knife skewer his heart. 'You would walk away from what we have?' he asked in a raw tone. This was crazy. Hang his pride. He would explain, and then she would stop looking at him as though she hated his guts.

The huskiness in his voice made Emma hesitate. He sounded as if he cared, sounded as if he did not want her to leave. But maybe her ears were deceiving her, and hearing what she wanted to hear. Rocco had lied to her—just as Jack had lied throughout their marriage.

'What *do* we have, apart from good sex?' She could not bear to think of all the other things they had shared. The fun and laughter, the long conversations and lazy after-noons making love. Clearly those things had meant more to her than to him. He had destroyed her trust, but she refused to let him see that he had broken her heart. 'There's nothing to keep me here.'

'Then go,' he said savagely, stepping back so that she could climb into the taxi.

He could not force her to have faith in him, and he would not beg. What was the point? he thought bitterly. He knew her heart would belong for ever to her dead husband.

Hurt, pride and a pain more agonising than anything he had ever experienced, made his voice harsh. 'If you leave, Emma, I won't come after you. It's your choice if you decide to end our relationship right now. I will not give you a second chance.'

Spring had finally arrived in Northumberland, and the garden of Primrose Cottage was ablaze with daffodils waving their golden heads in the breeze. It was a perfect day for the nursery school's trip to a local farm to see the lambs, Emma thought, remembering Holly's excitement this morning. The little girl had adapted quite happily to their old life in Little Copton, and although she had mentioned Rocco and Cordelia a few times she'd loved seeing her friends again.

At least she did not have to worry about her daughter or, for the time being, finding somewhere to live. The sale of the cottage had fallen through, and the owner had told Emma she was welcome to stay until new buyers were found. Aware that that might be some months away, she had decided to get on with weeding the back garden. She had arranged to return to her nursing post next week, but until then it was imperative she kept busy so that she did not have time to think.

The image of Rocco's furious face as she had told the taxi driver to take her to Genoa airport seemed to be branded on her subconscious, and his final words, delivered with such deadly finality, haunted her dreams.

I will not give you a second chance.

Why would she want another chance with a deceitful cheat? she thought bleakly. Throughout her journey to the airport and the flight back to England she had assured herself that she had done the right thing. For the past five days settling back into Primrose Cottage and ensuring that Holly was happy had taken up all her time, and she had managed to push Rocco to the back of her mind—at least until she was alone in bed at night.

The long hours of darkness were unbearable, she acknowledged miserably, as she knelt in front of a garden bed and attacked a clump of dandelions with a trowel. She missed him so much that there was a permanent ache in her chest, and doubts, like stubborn weeds, refused to budge from her head. Maybe there was another explanation for the identity of the boy who bore such a striking resemblance to Rocco. The child had reminded her of someone else, and after days of racking her brain she'd realised that he looked very like Giovanni—Rocco's brother who had died twenty years ago.

But what did that tell her? she wondered wearily. Rocco's son was bound to share a family resemblance. There was no escaping the fact that Rocco had a secret life he had not told her about. He had deceived her and made her feel a fool. Tears slid down her face and dripped onto her jeans. Even after Jack's death she had not felt this level of raw agony—as if a serrated blade had slashed through her heart.

She heard the creak of the side gate and hastily scrubbed her cheeks with her sleeve. Gossip spread like wildfire through the village, and the postman would be curious if he saw her crying.

But instead of a cheerful good morning, there was silence—even the blackbird in the apple tree had stopped singing. The hairs on the back of Emma's neck stood on end and she stood up and turned round, catching her breath as the ground beneath her feet lurched like a ship's deck in a storm.

Her voice wouldn't work properly, and eventually emerged as a rusty croak. 'Why are you here…?'

Her nemesis, the keeper of her soul, gave a grim smile. Rocco had had a speech prepared, but the streaks of tears on Emma's face and her tangible unhappiness had made him forget his words and forced him to acknowledge a simple, stark truth.

'Because I've discovered that I can't live without you, *cara*.'

She closed her eyes, as if willing him to disappear. But Rocco wasn't going anywhere. He walked towards her, his eyes lingering on the rounded shape of her breasts beneath her soft grey wool jumper. His woman. He had endured five hellish nights before he'd accepted that pride was a lonely bedmate.

He halted in front of her. 'Marco is my half-brother— my father's illegitimate son. Enrico's three sons all inherited his unusual eye colour.'

Emma's eyes flew open, and she stared at him helplessly as guilt ripped through her. *His half-brother!* That was why Rocco had pointed out that the boy she had believed was his son looked like his brother Gio. There was no denying it. Once again she had misjudged him. This time so terribly that she knew he would never forgive her.

'My father abandoned his Swedish mistress when she fell pregnant, and he had no contact with Marco until he was dying and asked me to find the boy,' Rocco explained quietly. 'I could not tell my grandfather while he was recovering from heart surgery. He is fiercely proud of the D'Angelo name, and I feared the shock of learning about his son's reprehensible behaviour could kill him. For months I have worked to build a relationship with Marco and win his trust. I wanted to tell you about him, but I had promised him I would not reveal his identity to anyone until he felt ready for me to do so.'

Emma stared at his handsome hard-boned face and her heart clenched. He looked drawn, his olive skin stretched taut over his sharp cheekbones, and she had a feeling that, like her, he hadn't slept or eaten properly since their bitter parting.

She bit her lip. 'I refused to believe Shayna when she told me the rumour that you had a son. I told her you were an honourable man—and I meant it,' she insisted huskily when he gave her a wry look. 'I trusted you—and that was hard for me. A huge step that at one time I was sure I would never take. When I saw you in Genoa with a beautiful woman and a young boy I felt devastated.' The memory brought fresh tears to her eyes, but she owed Rocco the truth and she forced herself to go on. 'I felt like I did when I found out about Jack.'

Rocco tried to ignore the corrosive burn of jealousy in his gut. 'I understand how deeply you loved him, and how much you still grieve for him. Learning of his death must have been shattering.'

'It was,' she said slowly. 'But it was made worse because a few hours before the news came that he had died in a fire I found out that he had been unfaithful throughout our marriage.'

Rocco jerked his head back in shock. 'Did someone tell you that?'

'His mistress.' Emma gave a humourless laugh. 'Kelly was one of a long list of women he'd slept with, but she was also one of my friends—which made it worse. She said she was telling me about Jack's affairs out of loyalty to our friendship. But she also revealed that Jack was planning to leave me and our unborn baby and move in with her. Apparently he had told her she was "the one", but he said the same thing to me when he asked me to marry him.'

'I thought your marriage was made in heaven,' Rocco said roughly.

She gave another pained laugh. 'So did I. The revelations about Jack's infidelity destroyed my fantasy that we were happily married, but I never had an opportunity to ask him why he had betrayed me. I don't think he can have loved me—the only person Jack was in love with was himself. After his death I realised that I had been in love with the *idea* of love, rather than actually with him. He was good-looking and charming—the original Jack the Lad. I was flattered that he chose to marry me, and I ignored his many faults.'

She sighed. 'But nothing can alter the fact that he died a hero. At his funeral, part of me was proud of him and part of me hated him.'

'*Dio!*' Rocco interrupted explosively. 'All this time I thought you loved him. You allowed me to think your heart belonged to him,' he said accusingly. Pain tore in his chest. '*Why*, Emma?' he demanded roughly. 'Was it to push me away?'

She was startled by the raw emotion in his eyes. She had no idea where this conversation was leading, but after the way she had misjudged him she owed him her honesty.

'Jack's parents were utterly heartbroken when he died.

I couldn't damage their pride in him by revealing that he had been a lying cheat. They show Holly pictures of him and tell her how he was awarded a medal for his bravery. For her sake, as well as Peter and Alison's, I will always keep up the pretence that Jack was the perfect husband.'

She dropped her gaze from his and stared down at the lawn. 'And it was safer to allow you to believe I still loved him,' she admitted in a low tone. 'You are the ultimate playboy, and I was determined to keep my distance from you.'

'I noticed,' Rocco said dryly. 'I have never met a woman as prickly and distrustful of my motives. And I admit you had good reason. My sole aim *was* to get you into bed. I was certain I did not want commitment—why would I when I had seen the fall-out of bitterness and acrimony in my parents' failed marriage and those of several of my friends? Sex was a game, and mistresses are not hard to come by when you are wealthy,' he drawled sardonically.

'I was never interested in your money,' Emma said quickly, hating the idea that he lumped her in with women like mercenary Shayna Manzzini.

He laughed softly, and lifted his hand to brush her hair back from her cheek. 'I know that. You are different than any woman I've ever met. Compassionate, caring, fiercely independent and totally unaware of your sensual allure. Is it any wonder that I was out of my head with wanting you, *mia bella*?'

Emma's breath hitched in her throat as he traced his thumb over her lips, and her heart jerked painfully beneath her ribs when he lowered his head so close to hers that his words whispered across her skin.

'I still want you, Emma. I can't eat or sleep or function without you. Come back to Portofino with me? I know you want me,' he said raggedly. 'I can see the desire in your eyes, and your body tells its own message.' He curled his hand around her breast and gave a satisfied smile when her nipple instantly hardened beneath his touch. 'I can make you happy, and Holly will love living at the Villa Lucia.'

Fierce longing burned inside her so strong that her body shook with the force of it.

'I can't.' She jerked away from him, fighting the temptation to succumb to his velvet-soft voice.

It would be so easy to agree. She knew he would sweep her into his arms, where she longed to be, and kiss her with his sensual mastery until she was trembling with a desperate need that only he could assuage. But there was Holly. She knew it wouldn't be right for the little girl, and her daughter's needs would always come first.

Rocco paled beneath his tan. He had not anticipated her rejection, and he felt as though he was teetering on the edge of an abyss of eternal blackness. 'Why not?' he demanded savagely. 'You've told me you're not still in love with Jack. Is there someone else?'

No.' There could never be anyone but him. 'But I can't be your mistress, Rocco. It wouldn't be fair to Holly. She needs long-term security, and I couldn't bear for her to regard your villa as her home only to be uprooted and upset when you grow bored with our affair—as you undoubtedly would,' she said painfully. It had been hard enough to walk away from him after a few weeks; it would destroy her to be forced to leave him some months in the future, when he no longer wanted her. 'You said yourself you don't want commitment.'

'I didn't think I did.' He caught hold of her shoulders and hauled her against him, holding her so tight that the air was forced from her lungs. 'Haven't you been listening to a word I've said?' He stared down at her, and Emma's heart turned over at the fierce emotion blazing in his eyes, the betraying, shocking glint of moisture that revealed his vulnerability.

'I love you, Emma,' he said in a driven tone. 'I don't want you to be my mistress—I want you to be my wife.'

She opened her mouth, but no words emerged, and he took advantage of her parted lips by covering them with his own and sliding his tongue between them in a kiss of hungry passion and fierce possession.

Emma clung to him and kissed him back, unable to hold back her frantic response or deny the emotions storming through her.

'*Tesoro,*' he said in a shaken voice when at last he lifted his head. '*Ti amo.* I will love you always and for ever. I never thought I would feel like this,' he admitted. 'I think I fell in love with you the first night we met—when I re-alised you were wearing that ghastly woollen hat Cordelia had knitted for you because you didn't want to hurt her feelings. I know you've been hurt, but I'm not Jack, and I swear I will love you and be faithful to you until the day I die.'

Icy fingers of fear gripped his heart when he saw the un-certainty in her eyes, and he crushed her tighter to him— as if by sheer force of will he could make her love him. 'I know I can be a good husband, and a good father to Holly. I can teach you to love me. Just give me a chance,' he pleaded.

Emma pressed her fingers to his lips, her heart aching as she realised that he wasn't sure of her. 'Of course I love you,' she assured him softly. 'I couldn't have made love with you if I hadn't felt it in my heart. But your grandfa-ther told me he will only hand over control of Eleganza to you if you marry an Italian bride. I know how much the company means to you...'

'It means nothing compared to my love for you,' Rocco

told her passionately, relief seeping through his veins that she was truly his. 'You are my world, Emma. Silvio can do what he likes with his company—although I suspect he will be very happy with my choice of bride. Especially as he will gain a gorgeous little great-granddaughter, and hopefully more great-grandchildren very soon.'

As his words sank in, joy unfurled in Emma's heart. She felt as though she had travelled on a long journey but now she was home, safe and secure in the arms of the man who was the love of her life.

'How soon were you thinking of giving Silvio great-grandchildren?' she murmured as Rocco lifted her and strode into the cottage.

His tiger's eyes gleamed with a feral hunger as he headed purposefully up the stairs to her bedroom. 'I think we should practise making babies right away, *cara*.' His heart thudded when he stared down into her smoke-soft grey eyes. 'I love you,' he said raggedly.

Emma smiled. 'And I love you. And, as we seem to agree on everything, it's going to be a perfect marriage.'

* * * * *

CLASSIC

Quintessential, modern love stories
that are romance at its finest.

EXTRA

COMING NEXT MONTH from Harlequin Presents®
AVAILABLE JANUARY 31, 2012

#3041 MONARCH OF THE SANDS
Sharon Kendrick

#3042 THE LONE WOLF
The Notorious Wolfes
Kate Hewitt

#3043 ONCE A FERRARA WIFE...
Sarah Morgan

#3044 PRINCESS FROM THE PAST
Caitlin Crews

#3045 FIANCÉE FOR ONE NIGHT
21st Century Bosses
Trish Morey

#3046 THE PETROV PROPOSAL
Maisey Yates

COMING NEXT MONTH from Harlequin Presents® EXTRA
AVAILABLE FEBRUARY 14, 2012

#185 ONE DESERT NIGHT
One Night In...
Maggie Cox

#186 ONE NIGHT IN THE ORIENT
One Night In...
Robyn Donald

#187 INTERVIEW WITH THE DAREDEVIL
Unbuttoned by a Rebel
Nicola Marsh

#188 SECRET HISTORY OF A GOOD GIRL
Unbuttoned by a Rebel
Aimee Carson

You can find more information on upcoming Harlequin® titles,
free excerpts and more at www.HarlequinInsideRomance.com.

HPECNM0112

REQUEST YOUR FREE BOOKS!

Harlequin *Presents*

PASSION GUARANTEED SEDUCTION

2 FREE NOVELS PLUS
2 FREE GIFTS!

YES! Please send me 2 FREE Harlequin Presents® novels and my 2 FREE gifts (gifts are worth about $10). After receiving them, if I don't wish to receive any more books, I can return the shipping statement marked "cancel." If I don't cancel, I will receive 6 brand-new novels every month and be billed just $4.30 per book in the U.S. or $4.99 per book in Canada. That's a saving of at least 14% off the cover price! It's quite a bargain! Shipping and handling is just 50¢ per book in the U.S. and 75¢ per book in Canada.* I understand that accepting the 2 free books and gifts places me under no obligation to buy anything. I can always return a shipment and cancel at any time. Even if I never buy another book, the two free books and gifts are mine to keep forever.

106/306 HDN FERQ

Name _____ (PLEASE PRINT) _____

Address _____ Apt. # _____

City _____ State/Prov. _____ Zip/Postal Code _____

Signature (if under 18, a parent or guardian must sign) _____

Mail to the **Reader Service:**
IN U.S.A.: P.O. Box 1867, Buffalo, NY 14240-1867
IN CANADA: P.O. Box 609, Fort Erie, Ontario L2A 5X3

Not valid for current subscribers to Harlequin Presents books.

**Are you a current subscriber to Harlequin Presents books and want to receive the larger-print edition?
Call 1-800-873-8635 or visit www.ReaderService.com.**

* Terms and prices subject to change without notice. Prices do not include applicable taxes. Sales tax applicable in N.Y. Canadian residents will be charged applicable taxes. Offer not valid in Quebec. This offer is limited to one order per household. All orders subject to credit approval. Credit or debit balances in a customer's account(s) may be offset by any other outstanding balance owed by or to the customer. Please allow 4 to 6 weeks for delivery. Offer available while quantities last.

Your Privacy—The Reader Service is committed to protecting your privacy. Our Privacy Policy is available online at www.ReaderService.com or upon request from the Reader Service.

We make a portion of our mailing list available to reputable third parties that offer products we believe may interest you. If you prefer that we not exchange your name with third parties, or if you wish to clarify or modify your communication preferences, please visit us at www.ReaderService.com/consumerschoice or write to us at Reader Service Preference Service, P.O. Box 9062, Buffalo, NY 14269. Include your complete name and address.

HPI1B

USA TODAY bestselling author

Sarah Morgan

brings readers another enchanting story

ONCE A FERRARA WIFE...

When Laurel Ferrara is summoned back to Sicily
by her estranged husband, billionaire
Cristiano Ferrara, Laurel knows things are about
to heat up. And Cristiano's power is a potent
reminder of his Sicilian dynasty's unbreakable rule:
once a Ferrara wife, always a Ferrara wife....

Sparks fly this February

HP13049

Louisa Morgan loves being around children.
So when she has the opportunity to tutor bedridden Ellie,
she's determined to bring joy back into the motherless
girl's world. Can she also help Ellie's father open his
heart again? Read on for a sneak peek of

THE COWBOY FATHER

by Linda Ford,
available February 2012 from Love Inspired Historical.

Why had Louisa thought she could do this job? A bubble of self-pity whispered she was totally useless, but Louisa ignored it. She wasn't useless. She could help Ellie if the child allowed it.

Emmet walked her out, waiting until they were out of earshot to speak. "I sense you and Ellie are not getting along."

"Ellie has lost her freedom. On top of that, everything is new. Familiar things are gone. Her only defense is to exert what little independence she has left. I believe she will soon tire of it and find there are more enjoyable ways to pass the time."

He looked doubtful. Louisa feared he would tell her not to return. But after several seconds' consideration, he sighed heavily. "You're right about one thing. She's lost everything. She can hardly be blamed for feeling out of sorts."

"She hasn't lost everything, though." Her words were quiet, coming from a place full of certainty that Emmet was more than enough for this child. "She has you."

"She'll always have me. As long as I live." He clenched his fists. "And I fully intend to raise her in such a way that even if something happened to me, she would never feel like I was gone. I'd be in her thoughts and in her actions every day."

Peace filled Louisa. "Exactly what my father did."

Their gazes connected, forged a single thought about fathers and daughters…how each needed the other. How sweet the relationship was.

Louisa tipped her head away first. "I'll see you tomorrow."

Emmet nodded. "Until tomorrow then."

She climbed behind the wheel of their automobile and turned toward home. She admired Emmet's devotion to his child. It reminded her of the love her own father had lavished on Louisa and her sisters. Louisa smiled as fond memories of her father filled her thoughts. Ellie was a fortunate child to know such love.

Louisa understands what both father and daughter are going through. Will her compassion help them heal—and form a new family? Find out in
THE COWBOY FATHER
by Linda Ford, available February 14, 2012.

Love Inspired Books celebrates 15 years of inspirational romance in 2012! February puts the spotlight on Love Inspired Historical, with each book celebrating family and the special place it has in our hearts. Be sure to pick up all four Love Inspired Historical stories, available February 14, wherever books are sold.

Discover a touching new trilogy from
USA TODAY bestselling author

Janice Kay Johnson

Between Love and Duty

As the eldest brother of three, Duncan MacLachlan
is used to being in control and maintaining an
emotional distance; as a police captain it's his job.
But when he meets Jane Brooks, Duncan soon finds
his control slipping away. Together, they fight for a
young boy's future, and soon Duncan finds himself
hoping to build a future with Jane.

Available February 2012

From Father to Son
(March 2012)

The Call of Bravery
(April 2012)